"Are you ready

"As ready as I'll ev . She responded with a w firm around his. The pro one, but he felt better with her by his side. "Kassia, you've been too good to me."

Too good. More than he deserved. He had to tell her not to wait on him or for him. "Kassia, I—"

"What is it?" She squeezed his hand. The comfort of her touch was so appealing.

The words wanted to form on his lips, but they couldn't. "I–I want to thank you—for being here."

TAMELA HANCOCK MURRAY is the award-winning, bestselling author of eight titles for **Heartsong Presents,** many novellas, and seven Bible trivia books. She shares her home in Virginia with her godly husband and their two beautiful daughters. They stay busy with church, school, cheerleading, Scouting, and work. Tamela hopes that her stories of God-centered romance edify and entertain her sisters in Christ. Contact Tamela by e-mailing her at TamelaWrites@aol.com

Books by Tamela Hancock Murray

HEARTSONG PRESENTS
HP213—Picture of Love
HP408—Destinations
HP453—The Elusive Mr. Perfect
HP501—Thrill of the Hunt
HP544—A Light Among Shadows
HP568—Loveswept
HP598—More Than Friends
HP616—The Lady and the Cad

Don't miss out on any of our super romances. Write to us at the following address for information on our newest releases and club information.

Heartsong Presents Readers' Service
PO Box 719
Uhrichsville, OH 44683

Or visit www.heartsongpresents.com

Forever Friends

Tamela Hancock Murray

Heartsong Presents

To my Momma, Ann Hancock
A Proverbs 31 Woman
The circle will never be broken.

A note from the Author:
I love to hear from my readers! You may correspond
with me by writing:

Tamela Hancock Murray
Author Relations
PO Box 719
Uhrichsville, OH 44683

ISBN 1-59310-477-4

FOREVER FRIENDS

*Our mission is to publish and distribute inspirational products offer-
ing exceptional value and biblical encouragement to the masses.*

All scripture quotations are taken from the HOLY BIBLE, NEW
INTERNATIONAL VERSION®. NIV®. Copyright © 1973,1978, 1984 by
International Bible Society. Used by permission of Zondervan
Publishing House. All rights reserved.

All of the characters and events in this book are fictitious. Any
resemblance to actual persons, living or dead, or to actual events
is purely coincidental.

PRINTED IN THE U.S.A.

Or check out our Web site at www.heartsongpresents.com

one

Her duties as a bridesmaid all but over, Kassia took a sip of hot apple cider and watched Lexie and Theo make the rounds talking to their guests. Being a part of their happiness had been the perfect way to celebrate New Year's Day. The North Carolina sun had shone all afternoon, though not too brightly. The outside chill permeated the reception hall, enticing some of the wedding guests to hover near the fireplace so they could enjoy the warmth of the bright flames.

Kassia sighed. Lexie was so lucky. Only she could plan a huge wedding and reception in the middle of winter and enjoy the cooperation of the weather. Of course, Lexie would attribute the perfect day to a blessing from God, but Kassia figured Lexie's good fortune could be attributed to simple luck.

Liz, Lexie's sister and matron of honor, nudged her. "She's getting ready to throw the bouquet. Go on up."

Kassia looked at a throng of women and young girls that included Lexie's five-year-old daughter, Piper. They clustered in the center of the reception hall, with Lexie standing only a few feet away. Shrieking and jumping up and down, they acted as though they believed the old superstition that the one who caught the flowers would be the next to marry.

The bridal bouquet toss was Kassia's least favorite part of any wedding. She wrinkled her nose. "Thanks, but I think I'll sit this one out."

Liz tugged on Kassia's elbow. "Oh no you won't! I'm going, too, you know. And anyway Lexie will never forgive me if I let you sit here and watch everyone else! Do you want to ruin your chance of finding happiness?"

"Who said I'm not happy now?" Seeming to have a will of its own, Kassia's gaze fell on Teague Boswell, one of Theo's groomsmen. "But maybe I shouldn't take any unnecessary chances with my luck." She set down her empty punch cup on the nearest table and headed toward the crowd of hopefuls.

Kassia reached for the bouquet of white roses and baby's breath amid forty or so other hands. The flowers became a blur of white and green, flying high over the crowd. She stretched her hands above her head and caught the cluster of flowers as several of the blooms brushed against her fingertips. Steadying the bouquet with the other hand, Kassia secured her prize. Squeals of delight ensued.

"You're next!" Liz teased.

Kassia shook her head. How could she, a complete and utter failure at finding love in the past and with no promising prospects for the future, be next to marry? "I doubt it."

"Are you so sure?" Liz tilted her head in Teague's direction.

Teague caught her gaze and sent her a charming grin, his eyes bright.

Feeling suddenly shy, Kassia pretended to examine the bouquet intently. In spite of her feigned disinterest in Teague, her heart fluttered.

Throughout the prenuptial celebrations for Lexie and Theo, Kassia had been paired with Teague, assigned to sit by him at the rehearsal dinner and walk down the aisle with him when the bridal party departed from the church after the ceremony. The pairing was no accident. She just knew it.

Deliriously happy with Theo, Lexie wanted to spread her joy to her friends. She wanted Kassia to find a good man and would stop at nothing to see her dreams for Kassia come true. She had to admit, Lexie knew her criteria for acceptable suitors. The sight of Teague's smoky gray eyes and honeyed hair, the sound of his smooth voice, the pleasant aroma of his citrus cologne, all made her want to be closer to him. She suppressed a gleeful sigh. No man had made her feel so wonderful by his mere presence since—well, since—never!

But despite all attempts to throw them together, Kassia was sure Teague was not available—in one way or another. Either he had a girlfriend no one knew about, or he was committed to his career, or he simply wasn't interested. No matter how many encouraging looks Teague threw her way, she knew he was out of reach.

With men that was the story of her life.

❧

Fresh from decorating Theo's car with shaving cream and a JUST MARRIED sign, Teague watched Kassia, clad in emerald green, catch the bridal bouquet then be teased and congratulated by the other women. He clapped along with the others. He couldn't remember another wedding with so many bridesmaids and groomsmen. Ten gorgeous bridesmaids looked more like a cast from a movie set than an assortment of friends and family. But none was lovelier than Kassia.

Teague wondered if Theo had paired him with Kassia on purpose. The two men had been friends since they had become study partners during a chemistry class in college. Theo knew he would be taken with Kassia's intelligence and sophistication. He was transfixed by her creamy skin that blushed like a ripe peach, her lithe figure, and dark curls. In his eyes she was a living doll.

She had been introduced as Lexie's best friend and roommate from college. Despite her rather ordinary introduction, her brunette beauty smoldered with mystery. He found himself wanting to know more. Teague couldn't recall a time when he was more intrigued with a woman. Any woman. Then again he hadn't tried to interest himself in a woman in a long while.

When did he have time? He had completed his advanced degree recently and landed a great job in the computer industry, his chosen field. How much more blessed could he be?

His boss was a driven, energetic entrepreneur. He couldn't pay Teague the salary he might have demanded at a larger organization. But the upstart company's long-term promise of fulfillment emotionally and financially made Teague jump out of bed with anticipation the moment the alarm clock rang each morning. Now, unencumbered with graduate school and situated in a small house he'd just rented, Teague felt he was in a position to offer a woman some stability and thus seek a wife.

He looked at Kassia and grinned. She averted her eyes, reminding him of a heroine in an old-fashioned book, or one of those silent movie stars in the films he caught on television occasionally after most normal people had gone to bed for the night.

Kassia Dahl just may be The One.

He had to take a chance. If he missed the opportunity now, she might slip out of his sights forever.

Since Kassia had become engrossed in conversation with one of the other guests, Teague took his time inching his way toward her—an easy feat since the reception hall was filled to capacity.

Finally he was close enough to her to take in the fragrance she had been wearing since they met. He thought he could identify her in a dark room just by her pleasant scent, now so familiar.

He tapped her on the shoulder. She turned to him. Now that he was looking her in the face, he was speechless. What could he say?

"Having fun?" he blurted. *Oh, now that was one brilliant question.*

"Everyone seems to think I should be. I caught this." She held up the white roses.

"I know. I saw you. You must have played softball in high school."

"Hardly. But I was pretty good at tennis."

"Me, too." Something else they had in common. That was a good sign. He rubbed the edge of his half-empty punch glass. "So have you gotten any marriage proposals yet?"

"Not yet. What's wrong with this crowd? You'd think at least one of the men here would get the hint, wouldn't you?" Her dark irises stared at him from the corners of her heavily lashed eyelids. "Unless that's why you wanted to see me."

"Of course. I'm just the first in line." He winked.

"I see." She looked over his shoulder and pretended to spot a long line of suitors. "You'd better make your offer good then."

He swallowed the rest of his hot cider, now lukewarm, allowing the burst of cinnamon and tinge of apple to fortify him with courage. "I'd like to. But I'm afraid it looks as if we won't be seeing much of each other after today."

Her mouth drooped with what he hoped was disappointment. "Oh, really?"

His heart raced. "Unless you'd like to change that," he added quickly.

"Well, I do live in Richmond." She paused. "And didn't you say you live in Amelia County?" She named a fast-growing area that, thanks to new development, was burgeoning into a popular outer suburb of Virginia's capital city.

"I sure do." He grinned. "So, considering this wedding is in another state, what's the probability we'd end up living so close together?"

"Considering that both Lexie and Theo live in Richmond, I'd say the probability is pretty high."

He couldn't help but chuckle. Yet her diplomatic response didn't give him much to go on. Was she being nice, or did she want to see him again once they returned home? There was only one way to find out. He had to ask her out to something. Anything.

Teague wished he had tickets to a concert or a sporting event. Now that he had broached the subject, he realized he had no idea what might interest her. What would be logical and safe? He racked his brain.

Ah. Dinner. Everybody has to eat. But where? He thought about the trendy places around town. The historic district was always a safe bet. But which place? He'd seen the menu posted on the window at the Berkley Hotel, and though their five-diamond restaurant was pricey, he'd always wanted to try it. "How about dinner at the Berkley Hotel?"

She let out a little gasp. "The Berkley? Wow! You go all out, don't you?"

He shrugged, hoping to conceal the fact that he was pleased he'd impressed her. "What else is money for?"

"You're right. I like a man who doesn't mind going to a nice place," she said.

"Good. Not that I go there every night, mind you."

Kassia laughed. "I would hope you wouldn't have to eat out every night."

He chuckled, not wanting to admit she had hit a little too close to home for him. Not that he ate in a restaurant every night. Even worse. He ordered carryout most nights, then took it either home or to the office to munch on mindlessly while he worked. He hadn't developed many cooking skills beyond boiling water for macaroni and cheese. Any woman who wanted a relationship with him would have to be a good cook. Or she would have to master at least meatloaf and mashed potatoes if she wanted to eat a home-cooked meal at the Boswell house.

Suddenly he realized Kassia was still looking at him. No wonder. He hadn't made the date and time firm. "I'll make reservations for next Saturday night then?"

"Perfect. I'll look forward to that."

He took out his wallet and withdrew a card. "Here're my address and phone number." Well, that had been easier than he imagined. A surge of confidence filled him. "You know something?"

"What?"

"The minute I saw you, I knew for sure the Lord had answered my prayer."

She stiffened. "Oh, really?"

Teague knew he shouldn't have blurted out such a strong sentiment. After all, he hadn't known Kassia long, not even out of her role of bridesmaid. What had he been thinking to drop the J-bomb so early? "I—I'm sorry. If you hang out with me long enough, you'll find I have a big mouth."

"I think I already have." Instead of being light, her tone was sharp, and her expression darkened.

Teague chuckled, but Kassia didn't take the hint and lift her own mood. She looked at the bouquet she held and fingered several petals of one of the roses.

"Now what did that poor little flower ever do to you?" Teague joked.

She pouted.

For an instant Teague was tempted to retract his offer for dinner. Why had the mere mention of the Lord brought about such a dramatic change in attitude and so quickly?

A sense of sadness engulfed him. He was all too aware of the Lord's instructions to take the gospel out into the world, and so he rarely missed an opportunity to be friendly to all types of people. But he would never consider a committed romantic relationship with a woman who didn't share his faith. Judging from her reaction, clearly Kassia didn't believe as he did. Not even close.

No. I'm a gentleman and a Christian. I won't go back on my word.

A silent prayer rushed through his mind. *Lord, help me to be pleasant when we go out. And let her see You in me.*

He forced himself to smile at her. "I'll look forward to Saturday night."

Her unenthusiastic nod did little to console him. He found

himself hoping that maybe she would find an excuse between now and then to cancel. Perhaps that would be the Lord's answer to his prayer.

❧

Moments after Lexie and Theo had departed amid a cloud of soap bubbles, the wedding guests retreated into the reception hall to enjoy more food and company. Kassia was in no mood to celebrate or talk to anyone. She snuck undetected into a small room in the church and slipped out of her bridesmaid's dress. Though she suspected the frothy number, with its long, puffy sleeves and a bow tied in the back, would never again see the light of day, she was careful as she hung it on a padded clothes hanger and slid a breathable cloth storage bag over it.

If only Lexie had been as careful about Kassia's feelings. How could her best friend have tried to set her up with someone who was such a religious fanatic? During the wedding activities Teague hadn't mentioned God at all. She had been led into a false sense of security, thinking he had a warm and fuzzy feeling about God, but not much more. But for him to tell her their meeting each other was an answer to prayer? She shuddered.

Then again what was she thinking? Lexie talked about God all the time. Theo entered the doors of the church every time they opened. She should have known any member of Lexie and Theo's wedding party would be an unabashed Christian. The type of raging, fanatical, maniacal Christian she'd seen all too often. The type of Christian who couldn't utter two sentences in a row without talking about God. Like her family, the family she rarely saw. Not that they missed her. They were too busy doing good, running to events for this worthy cause and that one, making a big splash at church. They never accepted Kassia's belief that you couldn't work your way into heaven—and never ceased to remind her she wasn't trying hard enough.

It only stood to reason that a devout man like Teague would not accept her either. Not a woman who was anything less than perfect.

Kassia left the reception and got into her car. Looking for a distraction, she found a rock music station on the radio and tried to take her mind off her angry thoughts as she made her way home. Yet after she arrived at her small apartment a few hours later, her mind revisited her ire as she unpacked her bridesmaid dress. She stuffed it in her already crowded clothes closet and reminded herself she needed to weed out her unwanted items and give them to charity. But she was in no mood to undertake such a big project at the moment.

With a huff, she headed to the refrigerator and opened the freezer door. Yes! The pint of chocolate chip ice cream was still there, waiting for her. The ice cream was one of many gastronomical indulgences she'd enjoyed during the dry spell since Brad dumped her after two dates. Two dates! That was a record, even for her.

Kassia took the ice cream out of the freezer and grabbed a soupspoon out of the drawer. Too angry even to look forward to it, she headed toward the floral-patterned couch and plopped down on her favorite spot. After turning on the television, she clicked through the channels until she found a show about interior designers transforming someone's living room, an expansive space that overlooked a mountain lake. Kassia wondered what it would feel like to own a living room that was bigger than her entire apartment.

As she watched the interior design team paint a large wall a loud shade of rusty orange, her thoughts returned to her beige walls, which reminded her of her own drab life, and then to Brad. She still winced when she remembered how he'd dumped her. She had desperately wanted a friend to share her defeat but couldn't talk about it with Lexie. She had made her disapproval of Brad known to Kassia. In a fit of spite fueled by the confidence that Brad was The Real Thing, Kassia had let Lexie believe she'd allowed Brad to become physical beyond a public display of affection. In truth, Brad bolted when Kassia refused him. She knew she put on a flirtatious front, a lingering behavior from her confused and uncertain teen years. Her habitual coyness resulted in men treating her the way she believed she deserved.

Scraping the bottom of the ice cream carton, Kassia resolved not to give away her heart too quickly in the future. And that included any relationship with Teague Boswell, groomsman extraordinaire.

Her thoughts turned to Lexie. She had led a charmed life. Lexie had a gift for finding—and keeping—good men. The husband who left her a widow had been the kind of man most women only dream about. Kassia knew the extent of her friend's loss, especially since Lexie's husband left behind their little girl, Piper, too. Lexie spent years grieving before she would open her heart to anyone else. But Theo was just as wonderful. Kassia sighed. How could Lexie land two great men while Kassia couldn't find even one? Her mouth twitched into a sardonic grin. If she could call Lexie on her fabulous honeymoon in the Bahamas, Lexie would tell Kassia that God was responsible for all the good in her life.

But was He really? Kassia wondered. She thought about God, the big man in the sky with a long gray beard and flowing white robe that she had accepted as a little girl. The God who gave her comfort and soothed her childhood fears didn't seem to answer her prayers now that she was an adult. No matter how often she prayed, or how fervently, He had never sent a good man—at least, not one who would be accepting of her and her lapsed faith. Maybe her parents were right. Maybe she wasn't doing enough to work her way into heaven—or at least into God's good graces.

Why couldn't she be as relaxed about God as Lexie seemed

to be? "I talk to God every day," Lexie once told her. "I feel such a sense of peace when I pray."

Lexie wasn't being self-righteous when she made the admission. Her friend was only trying to describe the spiritual benefits she felt from a close relationship with God. Kassia wondered how Lexie could talk to someone she couldn't see. How she could feel God's peace for herself.

Kassia wasn't sure about anything at the moment, not even if she wanted to see Teague again.

"Maybe I should give him a call and tell him the whole idea about going out to dinner was a mistake. He should forget he ever met me. If I did call and cancel the date, I'd be doing both of us a favor."

She picked up the cordless phone that sat on the table by the couch. Holding it in her hand, she stared at the number pad. Teague had given her his business card with his personal information written on the back. A short search through her purse and she would have the number—her ticket to putting them both out of any potential misery—misery sure to result from any connection she might form with such a devout man.

Or would it? Maybe the fact that she and Teague met and then his surprising interest in her were signs she wouldn't be unhappy after all. She remembered that strange and wonderful emotion she felt when their gazes locked. Was this God's way of telling her something?

She let out a huff and mentally slapped herself. Now she was thinking like Lexie!

An image of Lexie popped into her head. If Kassia broke her date with Teague, she would disappoint Lexie and her old friend, Theo. She had made a promise to Teague, and to break it would be nothing short of rude.

She placed the phone back in its cradle. "I made a promise, and I'll keep it. But there won't be a second date."

two

The following Saturday night, Kassia halfway watched a rerun on television as she waited for Teague to pick her up for dinner at the Berkley Hotel. This time she wasn't eating ice cream. She didn't want to spoil her appetite for what promised to be the best meal she'd had in quite some time. Plus she didn't want to take a chance on spilling anything on her outfit. She had changed her clothes three times until she finally settled on a long-sleeved red-and-black patterned silk suit with a mandarin-style jacket. Black heels with pointed toes dressed her feet. Her purse was a small black beaded bag in the shape of a fan.

Her goal in choosing the outfit was to say, "I'm happy to be going out with you to a nice place, but I'm not trying too hard to impress you. And I sure didn't go out and buy a new outfit just for this dinner." Which, of course, she had. She just hoped her choice would communicate the message she intended.

The high collar on the jacket, which was the equivalent of a slit turtleneck, would pass muster in any church. Teague couldn't think it was too daring. The oriental floral pattern was in good taste. Small embroidered flowers were hardly identifiable from a distance. The suit was too dressy to wear to work but not dressy enough for a formal affair. It was just right for dinner at an upscale hotel. She hoped.

Why am I agonizing so much and being so careful? Why should I be concerned about what he thinks? I'm not going to see him again.

Her lips tightened. Maybe she shouldn't have bothered to try to make any impression at all, even if he was taking her to one of the fanciest places she knew. Maybe a plain dress would have been a better choice. Rising from her seat, she was about to head for her bedroom and search her clothes closet when she heard a knock on the door. Too late. The red-and-black suit would have to do.

On her way to the door, she couldn't resist stopping to check her reflection in a convenient wall mirror. The woman staring back at her looked polished. Good. She grabbed the purse she'd left on the table under the mirror and extracted her small perfume bottle. One more spritz should do. She hoped he liked gardenia. The scent had just been introduced by her favorite cosmetic line. Taffy, the saleswoman who always helped her, had assured Kassia that gardenia was a classic scent that was coming back into favor. Kassia tested it on her wrist and decided she liked its statement—feminine but bold.

Confident she looked as nice as she could, Kassia was ready to meet Teague again.

❧

Teague shifted his weight from one foot to the other as he stood in the carpeted hallway in front of Kassia's green apartment door. He waited for her to answer his knock. What was taking her so long?

Maybe his secret wish had come true. Maybe she wasn't home. Maybe she had forgotten. Or maybe she had deliberately stood him up. He couldn't remember a time when he wished someone would leave him stranded on date night. This had to be a first.

He studied the bouquet of mixed flowers he had picked up at the grocery store. Maybe he shouldn't have brought flowers, but his good upbringing compelled him to be considerate under any circumstances. The blooms with their pink, yellow, and white faces stared at him with hope. If Kassia didn't answer the door, he would give the bouquet to a random woman on the street. The flowers were too pretty not to brighten someone's day.

Then again what if it worked out? What if Kassia turned

out to be everything he'd always wanted in a woman, and then some? After all, he had been attracted to her beauty the moment he met her at Theo's rehearsal dinner. And he had been encouraged enough by her interest in him to ask her out in the first place.

Since a small part of him had always been a dreamer, Teague had imagined what the evening might be like should Kassia prove to be the woman of his deepest desires. He tapped his chest and felt a piece of paper folded in the inner pocket of his blazer.

Lord, please lead me tonight.

He was about to knock on the door a second time when it whooshed open.

Kassia stood before him, a brunette vision in a high-necked shiny red-and-black suit that set off her light complexion. Her lips were coated with a shade of red too daring for his taste, but he had to admit the color worked with the outfit.

He noticed a heavy scent that reminded him of the floral fragrance his grandma wore. He sniffed the air and realized the overpowering aroma emanated from his date.

Well, Lord, if You don't want me to be attracted to Kassia, making sure she reminds me of Grandma was a good idea.

If only Kassia weren't such a vision—

"Are those for me?" She pointed to the flowers.

"Oh!" He handed her the bouquet and realized that in admiring her he had forgotten to present her with the token. "Yes. Yes, they are."

"Imagine that!" She chuckled.

He couldn't help but laugh in return.

"Come on in while I get a vase. Have a seat." She swooped her arm toward a comfortable-looking couch, then disappeared into the kitchen.

He wasn't sure they had much time to linger. Their reservations were for eight, and the hour was already well past seven.

He decided to remain standing.

Kassia reappeared and set the bouquet on the end table by the sofa. "Aren't they lovely? I'll think about you every time I see them."

"Maybe I should have brought silk then, so they would last longer."

"Speaking of silk, nice tie," Kassia noted.

Teague looked down at his chest and remembered he had worn his best tie, a geometric patterned red-and-black silk that went well with his charcoal gray suit. The color was similar to Kassia's dress, so he could see why she was pleased with his choice. "Oh, yeah. Thanks." He fiddled with the change in his pants pocket. "Nice suit."

She looked at her skirt as though trying to remember what she was wearing. "Oh, this thing? I'm glad you like it."

He made a point of consulting his watch. "I guess we'd better get going. I made our reservations for eight."

⁂

Now that Teague was standing before her, Kassia wished she had insisted on seeing a movie rather than going to dinner. Then they could have sat in a darkened theater, staring at a screen and munching on popcorn, not needing to talk. Not only that, but the movie itself would have provided a topic for conversation on the way home. A discussion about plot lines and actors would be much safer than anything such as religion—a topic Teague was sure to broach with her before dinner was over.

Still, the flowers had bought him several brownie points. Maybe she could just think about them should the topic of religion come up. She couldn't remember the last time a guy, especially on a first date, had been considerate enough to present her with a bouquet. The guys she usually chose were either too broke or too unconventional—or both—to bow·to tradition. Remembering the light scent of the flowers, such a special treat in the dead of winter, made her wonder about the wisdom of her previous choices. Maybe this traditional stuff wasn't so bad after all.

Or maybe Teague wanted something from her, something she wasn't ready to give. Maybe he was building up to an emotional commitment she had no intention of following up on. Or even worse, maybe he planned to witness about God to her all night, hoping to bring her back in line with the church. Tightening her lips, she vowed to stay on her guard. She would make it through the evening somehow.

During the brief car ride to the hotel, Kassia managed to keep the conversation directed toward passing sights in town. When they arrived at their destination, a valet opened the door for her then took Teague's practical blue car with the care one would give a limo. She hadn't even entered the building, and already she felt like a queen. Teague took her by the arm as they stepped into a lobby of understated elegance rather than ostentation.

The dining room was located only a few steps beyond the European-style hotel lobby, where they were greeted by a soft-spoken hostess. The room was dimly lit, with dark wood appointments. The diners themselves possessed a refined, sophisticated air. When Kassia peered in, she noticed almost every table was taken, but the crowd kept its conversation to a low and pleasant murmur. She glanced at the clothing the other women wore. She was relieved to see that her attire fit right in with theirs.

To Kassia's delight they were seated next to one of the many windows. She enjoyed watching people walking along the cobblestone street outside. Couples strolled by, hand in hand. Groups of friends dressed for a night out on the town loitered in front of the restaurant across the street. She didn't mind the fact that they could see her, too, dining with such a handsome man.

"I think I'll have the venison," Teague said, menu in hand.

"Deer meat? Isn't that a little adventurous?"

"If you want to try something different, this is the best place, don't you think?" he asked. "It's bound to be prepared properly here."

"True. But I think I'll stick with the filet mignon." Kassia swallowed. All of the selections were pricey, but to her relief Teague didn't do a double take or look distressed when he saw the menu. He must have known he was in for an expensive dinner when he asked her. She tried not to think of some of her other dates. Most of the men who had asked her out in the past would never have sprung for such an exquisite meal. She enjoyed being treated like a lady for a change. She realized she was smiling.

To her surprise he didn't speak once about spirituality as they talked through the salad course before dinner. Conversation flowed naturally as they learned more about each other.

"This is really good," Teague commented over his venison later.

She looked at the slices of meat drizzled in a rich brown sauce. "I have to admit, it looks better than I thought it would."

"Would you like to try some?"

She held up her hand. "No thanks. I'm not that daring." She nodded to her plate of beef and sautéed mixed vegetables. "You're welcome to try some of mine."

"I won't deprive you." He winked.

Despite their differing tastes in entrees, Kassia discovered over the course of the evening that they agreed on everything in life that mattered—except perhaps God's place in everyday affairs. She was thankful Teague didn't mention Him during dinner. Maybe he wasn't such a fanatic after all.

She didn't even mind talking about work with him, sharing anecdotes about her days as an office manager.

"I really enjoy my work," he confessed. "I managed to land

a job in my chosen field right after I got out of school."

"You're lucky. Most of the people I know are doing anything but what they majored in during college. But then again computers have been the up-and-coming thing for quite some time now. And I don't think that's going to change in the near future."

"I hope not. My boss, Will Herring, is great to work for. He just started his company, so I'm getting in on the ground floor." Teague spoke faster.

"You sound as if you can't wait to go to work every morning."

"That is exactly the way I was thinking about my job the other day."

"I hope you can keep your enthusiasm up to such a level as the years go by."

"I hope so, too," he said. "Sure, the job has its routine like anything else, but for the most part I can feel pretty creative. Right now I'm working on developing a new game."

"For personal computers?"

"Yes, although the company who contracted us might develop a game console system to compete with the others on the market."

"Wow! A new game!" Kassia drew in a breath with such force that the burst of air caused a little whistle to escape her lips. "That sounds interesting. I wish I had such talent."

"It takes more patience than talent—at least that's what I think. You just have to stick with it."

"Your game isn't too violent, I hope. Not that I'm meaning to be judgmental or anything," she added. "But it seems if you're really serious about being a Christian, you might want to think twice about putting out any computer games at all."

He cringed. "Ouch."

She looked at her plate. "I'm sorry," she muttered. "It's just that I've had some experiences in churches, and I know not everyone is as they seem."

❧

Kassia's opinion took him aback, but at least her expression of doubt helped him understand why she seemed allergic to Christianity. "But most of the people you encountered were dedicated Christians, weren't they?" Teague asked, hope rising in his voice.

"Sure, but it's the ones who weren't who seemed to be the most memorable."

"Isn't that always the way?" he agreed.

Teague concentrated on his food for a moment while he gathered his thoughts. His gut feeling told him Kassia had been led to him for many reasons. Surely one was for him to be the Lord's instrument in helping to counteract her negative view of Christianity. But how? He realized he had a long night of prayer and meditation ahead of him.

In the meantime, he decided to navigate the verbal waters into somewhat less murky territory. "Back to the issue of computer games, I didn't think you were being judgmental. I know the industry's been under fire lately about violent games. I have to say, a lot of the criticism is deserved. But you'll never believe what I'm working on."

"What?"

"Do you really want to know?"

"Sure," she said. "Unless it's an industry secret."

"I wish the industry as a whole valued what I'm doing that much." He grinned wryly. "I'm working on a Bible-based game."

"Oh! Sounds different."

"It's not totally different. Bible-based games have been released before and have sold well," he admitted. "I'm hoping mine's unique enough that it will capture mass-market attention."

"I'm sure it will. Good luck with it." Kassia took a sip of water.

"Thanks. I'm hoping for more than luck. I'm hoping that writing and selling this game is part of the Lord's plan for me."

"I'm sure anything you write will be an improvement over the violent and suggestive games on the market now," she told him.

"That's part of my goal in writing this. Of course, we're going for an *E* rating so everyone can play. That's one thing I appreciate about my boss. Not everyone would give me the latitude to introduce a Christ-centered game to a client. Some people I know would have laughed me right out of their offices just for suggesting such an idea."

"I think I can see why. I'm sure the market for Christian games isn't as broad as for secular games."

He nodded as he stirred two teaspoons of sugar into his coffee. "Sad, but true."

"I've shopped for computer games," Kassia said, "and have noticed a lot of them are either for teens or mature audiences. That makes it hard to buy many for little kids."

"Their parents would probably rather they play educational games anyway," Teague pointed out. "Little kids don't need to get lost for hours—or days—in a virtual world."

"True. It's hard to stop some games once you start. You start playing on a Monday; then you look at the clock, and it's—Thursday!" Kassia giggled. "I know Lexie wouldn't want Piper to get too involved in anything like that when it's better for her to play outside. And I always make sure she approves any type of game I buy for Piper."

"Good for you. She's lucky to have such a considerate friend."

~

The subject exhausted, Kassia looked into her cup of coffee and stirred it even though the sugar and cream had long since blended into the liquid. She enjoyed the brief silence as they waited for dessert to arrive.

"So," she finally ventured, "if you weren't working in

computers, what do you think you'd like to do?"

"You mean if I could clone myself and live several different lives all at once?"

"So you'd be a scientist?" she speculated before taking a sip of the warm beverage.

"No. I was just kidding about the cloning thing."

"Good!" She laughed.

"I think I might be a poet," he said.

She set down her coffee cup. "Really?"

"Is that so surprising?" He took a swallow of his own coffee.

She shrugged. "I don't know. I didn't have you pegged as a poet."

"But you could picture me as a scientist. I can't say I'm not flattered." He set down his cup, too, then leaned back and reached into the pocket inside his blazer to withdraw a folded sheet of paper. "Would you like to hear one of my efforts?" He began unfolding the paper.

"I take it I really don't have a choice," she teased.

"Sure you do." He folded the piece of paper and made a motion to return it to his pocket.

She reached over and tapped him on the hand. "No, don't do that. Of course I want to hear your poem."

"Are you sure?"

"Of course." She leaned toward him, placed her chin in her palms, and stared into his face. "Fire away."

"Okay. I was going to save this for after dinner, but since you asked, here goes." He read from the paper without looking up at her.

The Bridesmaid

A flash of green taffeta, a dress
With a bow that suggested a little girl
But complimented the shape of a woman.

> *A smile reminiscent of sweet sixteen*
> *But knowing, like that of a lady.*
> *A voice like pearls dropping on a mirror,*
> *Each word crisp and distinct.*
> *The bridesmaid who caught the bouquet,*
> *What are her dreams?*
> *Will they come true?*

Kassia took in a breath. "I don't know what to say."

"That is all you have to say then." The smile that crept onto his face bespoke his feeling of victory.

"I wasn't expecting anything like that."

"What were you expecting?" he asked.

"Oh, I don't know. Maybe a poem about a sunset or maybe God. But not what you just read. You're really talented."

"You didn't think I'd write about you?"

"No." She lifted the miniature pitcher of cream beside her cup and poured in a few drops, watching as the rich liquid whitened her coffee.

"I–I hope you don't think my poem is presumptuous in any way. That's not what I meant to be."

She set down the pitcher and looked up at him. "No, not at all. Really, I think what you wrote is quite sweet. Nobody has written me any poetry since"—she tried to remember—"since grade school. I'm touched by your gesture. I really am." She extended an open palm. "Will you let me hold on to the poem as a keepsake?"

"That's nice of you to say, but I really don't claim to be Shakespeare."

"You don't have to be. I'm so touched. You know something? I'm melting so much I can feel my body forming a puddle. I think my feet have already disappeared."

He chuckled. "Maybe you should have ordered ice cream to cool you off."

"Maybe so." She smiled. "I'll bet you write verses for all the girls."

"No, I haven't written poetry of any sort in a long time. They don't require computer geeks to know much about poetry in school," he quipped.

"You have a point. You've surprised me tonight on so many levels. I must admit, I saw you as more of a jock; yet you have the heart of a poet."

"I'm still not sure I'd quit my day job to write a book of verses."

"I'm not sure I'd advise anybody to quit their day job to be a poet, at least not until they got a regular gig." She chuckled.

"Poet laureate then?"

"That might be a start."

"Since I need to keep working at my nine-to-five, maybe I should start dressing the part of computer software programmer." Teague patted his shirt pocket with his hand. "I'd better remember my pocket protector from now on."

Kassia giggled.

Teague reached for his pants pocket. "Where's my duct tape? If I don't have a roll on hand, I won't be able to fix my glasses." He tapped his temple with his forefinger. "Uh-oh. Guess I left my glasses at home, too." He leaned toward her. "Could you drive us home? I can't see a thing without them."

By this time Kassia was having trouble containing herself. She couldn't remember the last time she'd enjoyed such good conversation.

"I don't care what you say, even with glasses and a pocket protector, I don't think you could look much like a computer geek."

"Thanks, but seriously, I'm glad we've come a long way from those old stereotypes."

"True. Nowadays just about everybody has to be computer proficient," Kassia said. "But I have to say, now you've made me wonder—does anyone still use a slide rule?"

"A slide rule? I'm surprised you even know what one is."

"Oh, I had a quirky professor who used one. Never did understand it." She smiled.

"I can't speak for everyone, but I haven't used one lately. Can I tell you something?" He cut his glance left and right, then lowered his voice to a whisper. "I do know how one works. I hope that doesn't scare you too much."

"Not too much." She was still chuckling when the waiter set a generous slice of chocolate cake with raspberry sauce before her.

As they concluded the meal, Kassia sat, relaxed. She marveled at how she was taking such pleasure in being out with a man. Teague was perfect. Almost too perfect.

Suddenly she wondered if Teague was telling the truth. She had seen her share of smooth men, including those who wrote poetry. Could he be pretending to be a Christian to hide a Casanova lurking inside? She erected a mental fence to protect herself.

She tried to keep the topic on safe ground. "Where do you get your inspiration for your writing?"

"In this case, from you, of course."

She laughed. "You're too sweet. I suppose you want me to think meeting me brought out the poet in you?"

"All right. I confess. I've been writing poetry for a while now. In fact I've always dabbled in it, at least since middle school."

"What was your inspiration then? Another girl, I guess? Should I be jealous?" She laughed.

"Never." He shook his head. "No, my inspiration is rarely a woman. It's usually the Bible."

"The Bible?"

"Sure. A lot of it is written in verse. Especially the Psalms."

Kassia searched her brain to recall long-forgotten Sunday

school lessons. "You're right." She felt her body tense. How had he managed to steer the conversation to his favorite topic so adroitly?

"So you know your Bible pretty well? Or are you just saying I'm right because you think it's what I want to hear? Not that I mind being told I'm right."

She found his grin irresistible. "No, I do remember a few things about the Bible. I used to go to church all the time."

"Used to."

"Don't worry about me. My parents were always active in their church. Still are, in fact. I don't think the doors open without their being there."

"Good for them. But remember, God doesn't have grand-children. He only has children."

"I know. I'm saved. I've been saved a long time. When I was a little girl."

"Really?"

"I asked Jesus into my heart when I was five years old."

"Me, too."

Kassia hoped her relief didn't show on her face. Now that she had told him she was saved, maybe Teague would take the pressure off and go back to being perfect.

three

Teague brightened when Kassia made her admission. If she came from a stable Christian home, surely she was saved! What more could he ask for in a woman?

Father in heaven, thank You!

For the first time since Theo's wedding, Teague allowed himself to drink in Kassia's beauty without a critical eye. Except for telling her about his Bible-based game, he had been reluctant to bring up the subject of religion, fearing her response might be negative. But when he saw the chance to mention the Bible in a personal way, he had to go for it. First her interest in his game and then her willingness to share her testimony had been a great reward for him. Finally he felt free to enjoy Kassia's company.

As he would with any person he was trying to get to know, he decided to probe a little into her past.

"I'll bet you were in your church youth group when you were a teenager," he ventured.

She nodded. "You guessed it." She didn't smile, but her jaw seemed to set in a firm line. He wondered why.

He cleared his throat. "I'm a youth leader at His Kingdom and Holiness Church."

Her eyes widened. "A youth leader? Wow! That's some commitment. Are you thinking of studying to be a pastor, too?"

"I'm afraid not, at least not at this point in time. Maybe that can be a second career when I'm older," he speculated. "But for now it's all I can do to work at my job, much less shepherd a flock, too. I leave that to Pastor Joseph."

"That's probably a good idea." She seemed to be lost in a

daydream for a moment. What was she thinking? She ran her finger over the rim of her coffee cup as if trying to memorize its circular shape. "I think you have to be certain you're called to the ministry before jumping in."

"Amen to that." He smiled.

She gave him a weak smile. "Kingdom and Holiness Church," she muttered. She glanced at the ceiling, thought for a moment, then looked at him. "Is that the brick church near the new shopping center south of town off Route 360?"

"That's us." He swallowed. Should he ask her or not?

"I always admire the stained-glass window when I go by. I like how it's lit up at night."

Her comment encouraged him. *Lord, I hope I'm doing the right thing.*

"Um." He hesitated. "Do you like to ski?"

"Well, that's quite a jump in subject." She grinned. "To answer your question, yes, but I'm not that good at it. I don't go often."

"Our youth group is planning a ski trip in a couple of weeks," he said.

"Sounds like fun."

"It always is. We've been going for three years now."

"You must be an expert skier."

"Not really. My family didn't have the money to splurge on such an expensive hobby when I was a kid, and the nearest slopes were over an hour away, so I learned to ski on these trips. You can be at any skill level from beginner to expert to go," he added.

"That's nice to include everyone."

He pursed his lips then wiped them with his cloth napkin. He was conscious of her watching as he folded it and set it back on his lap.

It's now or never.

"Uh," he finally said, "I–I was wondering, would you like to come along?" He glanced at her quickly then returned his gaze to his coffee cup.

"Me?"

"I don't see anyone else sitting at this table." He chuckled.

"True." She hesitated. "Are you sure? I mean, they don't mind that I'm not a member of your church?"

"Of course not. Lots of the kids are bringing friends from other churches and their schools, too."

"Well, as I said, I haven't been skiing in ages. I don't know how good I'll be."

Was the lack of confidence she expressed a real fear of looking foolish, or was she just trying to bow out gracefully? He couldn't tell. "It doesn't matter. I'm not asking you to teach or chaperone. Most of the kids don't go skiing that often, so they're at the beginner to intermediate levels anyway."

She paused for only a moment. "Well, all right then. I guess I can get up enough courage to go."

The smile that broke out on her face reminded him of a little girl who had just received a new doll for Christmas.

"Good!" Suddenly he remembered how rambunctious his youth group could be. "I have to warn you, though—you may not want to mention you're my friend. They might tease you."

"Should I pretend someone else invited me?"

"Hmm. That would be hard to pull off, wouldn't it?" He saw the silliness of his advice. "I hope you don't mind a little ribbing then."

"They're trying to get you hooked up with someone, huh?"

"They ask me about my love life every once in a while. I don't have much to tell them," he confessed. "I don't mind their questions, though. I know they just want me to be happy."

She swallowed and stared at the silver spoon resting on her saucer. "It must be nice to be involved with a group of teens who like you so much, especially since you're in charge of them."

"Sometimes I think they're the ones who are in charge of me."

"I understand things can get that way when you're dealing with teens." She flashed him a charming smile that showed off her straight white teeth.

He smiled back. Teague couldn't believe how well the evening had progressed. How had he gone from wishing Kassia would cancel their date, to asking her to accompany their youth group on a ski trip? He felt a vague sensation of floating.

He was brought out of his dream state by the smell of cheap men's cologne wafting nearby. Teague immediately fell back down to earth.

He looked up and saw a man had stopped by their table. His heart skipped a beat. Whoever this man was, his were the type of good looks that filled other men with envy and made women swoon. Sort of like Kassia. She swayed back and forth as though she was about to faint, though she seemed to be doing her level best to hide the man's effect on her.

"So, Kassia," he was saying. "Long time, no see."

She looked up at him briefly then returned her gaze to her half-eaten chocolate cake as quickly. "Yep."

"I miss seeing you around. Where have you been hiding?"

"Nowhere much." Kassia shifted in her seat. "I've been busy. Uh, Brad, this is Teague."

Teague simmered in spite of himself. No last name, huh? Just Brad. Come to think of it, Kassia seemed to forget Teague had a last name, too.

So who was Brad? A colleague at work? Her supervisor? Someone from her neighborhood? A friend from some sort of organization? Even worse, her boyfriend? Surely Kassia wouldn't agree to see Teague if she already had a boyfriend. Yet the way he set his hand on the back of Kassia's chair bespoke a confidence that seemed territorial—more territorial than Teague liked.

Brad glanced at Teague as if he were no more than an annoying fly. He leaned toward Kassia and kept his eyes focused on her, a ploy Teague was sure he used just to keep him from joining the conversation.

Irritated, Teague studied Kassia's body language. To his surprise and pleasure, he noticed that no matter how far Brad leaned over, she inched just as far away. If Brad was Kassia's boyfriend, a breakup was sure to follow soon.

"So, Brad," Teague managed to say, "don't you have someone waiting for you?"

Brad shrugged. "Just the soccer team. We're here for our end-of-season get-together."

"End of season?" Teague questioned. "The fall season should have ended weeks ago. Besides, I would have thought a pizza joint would have been the place for a sports celebration."

"For one, the fall season did end awhile back. We just couldn't set a date sooner because of the holidays. And two," Brad said, "we go out for pizza all season. We're here tonight because our coach is moving to another state, and we're saying good-bye to him. Not that I owe you any explanation."

"You don't," Teague admitted, "but you'll have to explain to your team if you don't get back to your party. I'm sure they miss you."

"I'm sure." He shot Teague an unpleasant look from narrowed eyes then studied Kassia with a more friendly expression.

Kassia downed the rest of her coffee without saying a word. Tension sat beside them as surely as any dinner companion could have. Teague waited for Kassia to elaborate on her relationship with Brad; instead she stirred sugar into her coffee as though the procedure required as much care as brain surgery.

"How dare that guy stop by and talk to you!" Teague's brows furrowed; then he winked. "I can't believe you had a life before you met me last week!" He waited, hoping his levity would diffuse the anxiety she was apparently feeling.

"I wish I could laugh about Brad. We recently broke up." She looked out the window at a couple strolling by.

"Oh." So Brad did mean something to Kassia. He couldn't keep disappointment from coloring his tone. "How recently?"

Kassia looked at the ceiling as she apparently made a mental calculation. "Before Lexie's wedding. Not too recently really. And let me make another correction," she added, looking him in the eye. " 'Broke up' is too strong a phrase. We weren't serious. We'd only gone on a couple of dates."

"But it hurt when he left." His voice was quiet.

"More than it should have, I guess." She traced an imaginary figure on the white tablecloth with her red fingernail.

"Don't worry. I know it's a cliché to say this, but it's his loss."

"Thanks." Her smile was bittersweet.

"I know it's never any fun to feel rejected."

She stopped tracing and looked up at him. "You must be kidding. Someone like you knows what it's like to feel that way?"

"What makes you think I'm immune?"

"Well." She leaned back and gestured at him with her palm open. "Just look at you."

Though not prone to blushing, Teague felt his face grow warm. "I appreciate the compliment, but it's not as if women throw themselves at me then beg to hang on forever."

Kassia grimaced and folded her arms.

Seeing Kassia's disbelief, Teague decided to take a chance. "I haven't had a real relationship—I mean a romantic one— since high school."

She unfolded her arms and leaned toward him. "You're kidding."

"No, I'm not. See? I told you I was a computer geek." He laughed, but the sound was more nervous than he would have liked.

"What was she like, this girl from high school?"

"She was a nice girl from church. Pretty and popular. We were one of the known couples around school," he said. "We thought we'd get married someday. But it didn't work out that way for us."

"I'm sorry. What happened?"

"I'd like to say I broke it off with her. But, to be honest, she broke it off with me."

"I'm sorry."

He shrugged. "Thanks, but it was for the best."

"Let me guess. She met someone else."

Teague's heart felt pain for a moment. How could Kassia have guessed so easily? "Yes. We went to separate colleges, and I must have seemed too dependable and too old hat for her once she met all those new guys. Thanksgiving break was the first time we saw each other after leaving for college. I was so happy to be going home and seeing her. But by then she told me she had moved on to greener pastures. I was heart-broken, but I couldn't do anything."

"Wow! She didn't waste much time."

He shrugged. "I wasn't the only one in my dorm. The same thing happened to my roommate that year. Apparently it's sort of a freshman tradition to dump your old high school boyfriend at Thanksgiving or Christmas break."

Kassia was silent for a moment. "Come to think of it, that happened a lot at my school, too. That's one time I escaped hurt, though. I didn't go to college with a boyfriend back home. But breaking up isn't a very nice tradition, in my opinion."

"But maybe it's a healthy one. If a woman doesn't think she's right for me, I'd rather find out before we're married than after."

"True." Kassia sighed. "Do you know what happened to your old girlfriend?"

"I haven't heard anything about her recently. She dropped

out of school and moved to the West Coast. All I can say is, I hope she's happy now."

"It's good you can be so forgiving," Kassia observed.

"I have no reason to wish her ill. That was a long time ago."

"Maybe one day you'll have the satisfaction of going to your high school reunion and showing her how successful you are."

"Yeah, right." He knew his lack of enthusiasm was evident. He hadn't been successful at all. At least not in the love department. Not with a relationship that was deep and meaningful, the type of relationship he wanted with a special woman.

"What do you mean, 'Yeah, right'?" she ventured. "Of course you're successful. Think about it. You went to a great university, and now you have a wonderful job with what sounds like the ideal boss. She should be proud to know you."

Now that Kassia mentioned it, perhaps he was pretty successful. "You think?"

"Yeah. I think." She nodded.

"Some people might disagree. I was upset when she broke things off, and I was tempted to go out and have a wild time. I admit it. I'm only human. I'm glad I didn't succumb to temptation, though. I couldn't have done it without the Lord's help."

"So you had women throwing themselves at you every day once they found out you were back on the market, huh?" Her tone was only half-teasing.

How could he tell her the truth—that many women had made him offers that were difficult to refuse—without sounding like a conceited jerk?

"Um, well. . ."

Kassia's laugh tinkled like a small set of silver wind chimes caught in a gentle spring breeze. "I know you're good-looking. You don't have to be modest." Her mouth set itself into a serious but gentle line. "You're serious, though? You stuck to your principles in spite of all those women?"

"Yes, I did. I'm keeping myself pure for my future wife."

Kassia's mouth dropped open. "You're joking, right?"

Teague hoped his disappointment in her reaction didn't show on his face. "I don't know of any guy who'd joke about a thing like that."

"Good for you. Now I have a confession to make." She leaned closer to him. "I took the 'True Love Waits' pledge when I was a teenager."

"You did? Then why are you so shocked about me?"

"I don't know. Maybe it's because my parents insisted I had to take it," she said.

"Really?" Teague wondered what kind of parents would force their teens to make such a serious commitment under duress.

"They're pillars of my church back home, and I think they thought it would look bad on them if I didn't go along," Kassia explained, as if she had read his mind. "They made my sisters, Deidre and Mona, take the pledge, too."

"They made all of you take it whether you meant it or not?"

"You could say that." Kassia grinned wryly. "How many brothers and sisters do you have?"

"Just one sister, Tabitha. She's the light of Dad's eye. She's younger than I am, but she makes more money. She started her own business."

"Good for her. What kind of business?"

"She owns a trendy little boutique."

"Oh, sounds like fun. What does she sell?"

"Her favorite description is 'an eclectic selection for today's woman.'" He recalled the last time he'd visited Tabitha's store. "She even has matching outfits for moms and daughters."

"That sounds sweet."

"Yeah, if you like that sort of thing." Teague shrugged. "She sells funky jewelry, too. Each piece is one of a kind, handmade by artisans."

Kassia's eyes widened. "Sounds neat." She touched her ear

and revealed a red hoop. "Earrings?"

"Lots of them. And things like pins and hair barrettes. Oh, and she carries trinkets. Gift items and collectibles."

"That sounds like a fun place to shop."

"Yes, but it's a lot of work. She wants to open a second store in either Old Town Manassas or Old Town Fredericksburg."

"You must be proud of her."

"I am. And you know what? I attribute some of her success to her taking the pledge many years ago."

"Really?"

"I sure do. That's because she concentrated on her school-work and stayed focused on her academic career instead of getting involved with a boyfriend too early."

Kassia thought for a moment. "I can see what you mean. At first I didn't want to take the pledge, but after I got in the pro-gram I could see it was a good idea for a lot of reasons. It had some immediate benefits, as you said. I didn't have as many troubles and worries in high school since I limited my involve-ment with guys. Except I wasn't as popular as some of the other girls." She set her chin in her palms.

When she moved, a whiff of floral perfume wafted his way. As the evening progressed, Teague had noticed the scent was reminding him less and less of his grandmother.

"That kind of popularity is false. And it's temporary at best," Teague pointed out.

"I can tell you're a youth leader." She chuckled.

"I try, but I can't promise how well everyone listens." He reached over and squeezed her hand. "But I'm glad you lis-tened, and I'm glad you've kept your pledge."

"Me, too. But isn't it harder for guys?" she wondered aloud. "Don't you have a lot more pressure?"

"Maybe. Sounds like a good excuse anyway."

"I don't regret not having as much experience as the rest of my single friends. I call myself 'Queen of the Dumpees.' "

"Queen of the Dumpees? What kind of name is that?"

"Can't you guess? I find a guy I like, he acts interested for one or two dates; then when he doesn't get what he wants, he dumps me. That's what it means." She let go of his hand and patted her lips with her napkin. "I shouldn't have said that. Now you'll think I'm a loser."

"I don't think you're a loser." Teague wasn't lying. Though Kassia was no loser, clearly she suffered from low self-esteem, caused no doubt by the trouble she'd had in past relationships. He cut his glance to Brad's table on the other side of the room. "That Brad guy is the loser in my book. He could only talk to you for a few minutes, but I have you for the whole evening."

He was rewarded by her smile.

"Your smile is so pretty. Were you ever in any beauty pageants?" he asked.

"Me? No way." She snickered.

"Too bad. You would have won. Seriously."

"Thanks for the compliment, but there's no way my parents would have let me prance around on a stage in a bathing suit."

"I have to admit, I can see the wisdom of that," Teague said, "especially since they made you take a purity pledge."

"I never was much of a performer anyway," Kassia informed him.

"Still, I'll bet you're the pride of your family."

"I wish." Her face fell slightly. "We're not that close. At least, not anymore."

Teague wondered what she meant. Based on her descriptions, Kassia's home sounded like the idyllic picture of a Christian family. Her admission bothered him. What had happened? He wished he could ask, but Kassia's closed lips and the cold light in her eyes told him not to.

When he pictured the woman of his dreams, Teague thought of someone close to God, not just in her past, but in her present and future. He'd wondered how pure Kassia could be when she seemed so worldly.

Lord, I know Kassia and I have seen each other only at Theo's wedding and now at dinner tonight, but I still feel a strong connection with her despite my doubts. Could this be the woman You want me to see?

The uncertainties left him searching for direction. He knew that waiting on the Lord was not acceptable for most people in this modern world. They wanted quick answers measured in Internet terms of microseconds. Teague was more patient. He knew in his heart he had to stay on good terms with Kassia until God showed him His purpose.

After dinner, they waited in the hotel lobby for the valet to bring Teague's car. Standing with her, a beautiful vision scented with gardenia, he discovered he hoped she would be in his future for a long time.

four

The following Monday, Kassia was surprised when Brad stopped by her office. She had thought surely her unenthusiastic reception toward his impromptu visit and Teague's brusque good-bye at the restaurant the previous weekend had been enough to discourage him, but apparently she had been wrong.

Brad worked in a different department from Kassia, and his duties never necessitated a trip by her desk. Obviously he had made a special trip to see her. What could he want? An uneasy feeling coursed through her. He hadn't noticed her since their breakup, at least, not until he saw her at an upscale restaurant with another man. She had the distinct impression that if their chance encounter hadn't happened, Brad wouldn't have sauntered into her small gray office as though he were her supervisor, and he wouldn't be leaning over her desk at this moment.

Although she felt his presence in the room, she didn't look in his direction.

"Hi, Kassia. What's the latest news with you?" he asked.

She glanced up long enough for him to know she noticed his presence, then returned her attention to her paperwork. "Nothing much. I'm just busy with all these papers." She chewed on her pencil with her front teeth, the yellow paint and soft wood easily giving way to the pressure.

He leaned in closer to her. She became conscious of his cologne. She enjoyed the pleasant musky scent, but she preferred the citrus fragrance Teague had worn on their date.

"It was nice seeing you the other night." Brad placed his

palms on the edge of her desk and paused as though awaiting a response.

"Hmm." She moved her chair as far away as she could then tapped her pencil on her desk. The phone rang, and she answered it without excusing herself.

He was still there after she transferred the call to accounts receivable, still leering at her. "A couple of the guys at my table remarked about how beautiful you looked, and I have to agree."

She did her best not to respond favorably to the seductive purr in his voice. To that end she kept staring at her paper. "Thank you. Um, I hate to be rude, but I'm really busy right now."

"I'll make it quick then, if I can have your attention."

Kassia sighed to show her exasperation and leaned back in her seat. She deliberately crossed her arms to indicate her lack of receptiveness to whatever he had to ask.

Undeterred, he gave her his most charming smile. "I was wondering if you might like to get together for lunch one day this week."

She didn't want to admit, even to herself, how tempted she was by his offer. Maybe going out to eat with him wouldn't hurt anything. After all, it was only lunch, and she would have to grab a midday meal somewhere. She looked into Brad's eyes and saw a sparkle of genuine interest.

She glanced quickly back at her paper then set her gaze on her black cylindrical pencil holder filled to the brim with writing implements, emery boards, and scissors. No. She couldn't go. This was a man she couldn't trust. Another call interrupted her, so she didn't have to answer right away.

"We could have a nice time," Brad persisted after the call was finished. "Unless you're too tied up with that guy you were with. What's his name—Teak?"

She looked him full in the face, keeping her tone cold.

"I think you mean Teague."

He stood upright and snapped his fingers. "Oh yeah. I knew it was some off-the-wall name like that."

"I happen to think it's a very nice name," she blurted with more emotion than she intended.

He held up both palms as if trying to hold off an angry lion. "Okay, okay. I didn't mean to offend your boyfriend."

"He's not my boyfriend." She nodded to the ringing phone and answered it.

No matter how many calls interrupted his invitation, Brad didn't seem to give up. "Well, then, he shouldn't mind if we have lunch together." He put a hand in his pocket and struck a pose. "So what do you say?"

Out of politeness she pretended to mull over his invitation. Then she braced herself by putting on an unsmiling expression to show she was serious. "Thanks for the offer, but not this week." She stared at the papers. The words blurred into a mass of gray.

"How about next week?" she heard him say.

"I can't," she said without looking up.

"You can't?" His tone was not unlike that of a top student expressing shock at receiving a failing grade. Then he curled his lips into a knowing line. "I get it. You're still mad because movie night didn't work out that time. Look—I'm sorry about that. I have to say, that friend of yours, what was her name— something like the car—Lexus?"

"Lexie."

"Yes, that's it. Lexie. Anyway she always stared at me like I was covered with anthrax or something. She's not still living with you, is she?"

"No, but that doesn't change anything."

He leaned closer. "Are you sure you can't forgive me?"

"Forgiveness is not the question here. The fact is I just can't see you right now." She kept her expression and tone firm as she returned her attention to his face. "I just can't. In fact I'm tied up for the next few months. Work has gotten crazy."

"Oh, really?" he scoffed, folding his arms. "That excuse might hold water with someone outside the office, but this is me you're talking to. I know the quarterly reports aren't due for two more months."

"But I make it a policy to stay on top of things rather than push through a mad rush at the last minute." She shrugged and flashed him an innocuous grin. "That's just the way I am."

For emphasis she straightened a wayward stack of papers and placed them in her "in" box, all the while fighting to ignore the personal magnetism he exuded with little effort. No matter how attracted she felt to Brad, she refused to reignite any relationship with him.

"I'm glad to hear you're such a conscientious worker. The company is mighty lucky to have you." Sarcasm dripped from his voice.

"Thank you." Her sarcastic tone matched his. "If you'll excuse me." She cleared her throat and looked toward the door.

"Okay. I can take a hint. See you around." He exited without further objection.

Content that she had finally gotten the message across to him, Kassia allowed herself a sigh of relief and returned to her work in earnest.

❧

That evening the phone rang as Kassia was finishing a meal of leftover Chinese takeout consisting of a few morsels of sweet-and-sour pork and a half container of fried rice. With a hurried motion she wiped her lips with her paper napkin and rushed from her dining room table to answer the phone in the living room.

"Kassia?"

The voice was unmistakable. Her stomach flipped like an Olympic gymnast. "Hi, Teague!"

"I'm glad I caught you at home. I hope I didn't interrupt your dinner or anything."

"You didn't interrupt anything important."

"Good. Hey, I want you to know I'm looking forward to the ski trip, if you haven't changed your mind about going."

"Of course I haven't chickened out. Once I make up my mind, you're stuck with me."

"Good. I wanted to fill you in on the details."

"Great. Let me grab a pencil." She leaned over and fumbled through several bills waiting to be paid and a letter from an old chum, finally discovering a pen at the bottom of the stack. She found space on the back of the water bill envelope to write down the information. An image of Lexie popped into her head. She would have already paid the bills and filed them away long ago.

Kassia smiled and concentrated on her caller. "Okay. Ready."

Somehow Teague could make the mundane minutiae of planning a trip seem intriguing. She wished he'd called to ask her out again before they were scheduled to depart, but she could appreciate that he didn't want to seem too eager or move too fast. He was proving himself a gentleman, and she found herself wanting more of his company.

Floating as she hung up the phone, she returned to her lukewarm meal, not even minding that the rice had gotten sticky in her absence.

The phone rang again. Maybe Teague had meant to ask her out for a second date but forgot. She skipped toward the phone.

"Hello?"

"Well, hello yourself!"

Her heart seemed to fall into her toes. "Brad." Her voice, lilting seconds before, now sounded flat to her ears.

"Is this a bad time? I can call back." His voice was as smooth as she would have expected from a close friend, not from a man she had rejected only that afternoon.

She resisted the temptation to put him off, which would only delay the inevitable. "No, that's fine. Now is as good a time as any."

Surrendering, she sat down on the couch and put her bare feet on a short stack of magazines that sat on the coffee table. She noticed she'd spilled a drop of red sweet-and-sour sauce on the knee of her gray sweatpants. At least they were old enough that she didn't care.

Her sweatpants weren't the only object of her indifference. How could she tell Brad no time was good for him to call? Not long ago she would have welcomed the sound of his voice. How much everything had changed!

Why couldn't he have called on the days he originally said he would? She remembered one Saturday in particular when she'd spent the better part of the day waiting for his call. She had stayed home then made sure her cell phone was on at all times, in hopes he would try to contact her. But no call came. Now here he was, stopping by her desk in the afternoon and calling again that night.

She listened as he flirted and tried to cajole her into giving him another chance. If he had realized how much a call from him would have meant to her in the past—but knowing him it might not have mattered anyway. He wouldn't have been reduced, though, to nearly begging her to go out with him now.

She knew what had changed his attitude toward her. Seeing her with Teague. Teague was a handsome man, no doubt about it. Brad saw him as a rival, competition to be squelched.

"Are you sure you can't put aside your other commitments and spend an hour or two with me?"

"Sorry, no."

"You know," he persisted, "we can sneak out for a long lunch on Friday. I can put in a word with your boss. She won't mind. I can tell her we're discussing business. I know a great little place that hardly anybody else has discovered yet. They have the best Italian food you ever put in your mouth. I know you'd like it."

"Maybe I would enjoy eating there sometime, but I can't," she insisted, twisting the beige phone cord. "And anyway, my boss would never believe you and I have any business to discuss—unless you were trying to hire me to work in your division. And I know she wouldn't excuse me for a long lunch just so she would lose me, as immodest as I know that sounds."

"I know you're a good worker," he said. "You've already told me more than once. But hiring you away, now that sounds like a good idea."

The thought of working in Brad's division made her stomach lurch. "Never mind that. I have no interest in working for your division. I like where I am. Thanks anyway."

"Oh, all right. So you want to play hard to get. I understand."

"No, you don't," she said. "I'm not playing games. I mean what I say."

"I'll take a no for now if you insist," he said, "but you don't need to worry. I'll still be around."

"Is that so? Well, don't hold your breath. I'm busy and not just with work." She took in a breath and prepared to drop what she hoped would be the verbal equivalent of a stop sign. "Teague and I are going on a ski trip in a couple of weeks."

"Oh." His voice sounded as deflated as a flat tire. "A ski trip? Where to?"

"Oh, up in the mountains."

"Is that so? I never would have guessed. I thought you would be skiing at Virginia Beach."

"Cute." She grimaced even though Brad wouldn't see her. His sarcasm was becoming annoying.

"What mountains?" he pressed.

"I'm not sure exactly where." She decided not to add that they'd be with a church youth group. If Brad wanted to think

the trip was something romantic, then that was his own fault.
Besides, she had to discourage him any way she could. "I've
got to run. Good-bye." She hung up the phone and hoped he
wouldn't call back anytime soon.

જ

Teague stared at the calendar on the wall of his work cubicle.
Snow-covered mountains reminded him of the weekend he
anticipated more than any other ski trip in recent memory.
The workdays that used to pass so rapidly now seemed to
move as slowly as standing water.

No matter how much Teague tried to concentrate, the
equations written on his paper didn't coordinate. He hadn't
made much progress on his work. In fact he hadn't made
much progress on anything. Not since that night with Kassia.
When he wasn't thinking about the ski weekend, his date
with her lingered on his mind, regardless of what he was
doing. She was mysterious, no doubt. She seemed to be
standing on the fence, wobbling with such uncertainty that
she could tip off and land on either side. Revelation 3:16 shot
through his brain: *"So, because you are lukewarm—neither hot
nor cold—I am about to spit you out of my mouth."*

Despite his eagerness to go, he was not without anxiety.
What would she be like on a ski trip with a bunch of rambunctious youth? While many of them were strong in the
faith, others weren't. Every teen in his youth group needed to
be around adults who would set a Christian example. And
they all had sharp radar for spotting hypocrisy. He didn't
expect Kassia to react negatively to their beliefs since he had
warned her she would be among church people, and her
background meant she would have an idea what type of
behavior would be expected of her.

If anything, he wondered if she might try to make them
believe she was enthusiastic about the Christian faith. But if
they sensed she was pretending to be a better Christian than

she was, they would chew her up and spit her out. As shaky as she seemed, Teague knew Kassia didn't need any confrontations or negative experiences during the trip.

His conflicting thoughts left him confused.

Lord, I pray I haven't made a mistake in inviting Kassia on the ski trip. I pray I haven't made a mistake in associating with her at all. Lord, show me the way concerning this woman.

At that moment his boss tapped him on the shoulder. "Teague."

He jumped an inch out of his seat.

"Sorry," Will apologized. "I didn't mean to scare you."

Teague regained his composure. "No problem. I was just deep in thought."

Will nodded. "If you can spare a minute, I need to see you in my office."

Will's expressionless face indicated the news couldn't be good. Maybe he was going to give Teague an assignment he didn't want. Teague could think of at least one dreaded task. He hoped Will didn't want him to help the new intern get the bugs out of a calendar and address book program that had proven to be a pill from the moment they started writing it.

Or maybe Will wanted to caution Teague about his lack of output for the day. If so, the warning would be justified. He rose from his seat and followed Will to his office. On the way, he thought about what he would say in his defense.

Moments later, shutting the door to Will's office behind him, Teague was about to apologize when his boss spoke.

"Grab a chair," he offered as he took his own seat behind the modest yet oversized desk. "Although this will take only a moment."

Teague complied, situating himself in one of the two stiff wooden chairs in front of Will's desk.

Will leaned back in his padded gray executive chair and clasped his hands as if the gesture would help him form his next sentence. "You know how much I value your work here, Teague."

"I think so." Good. The news couldn't be so awful then. Maybe he was planning to let some of the other people in the company go and needed Teague's help with the transition. He decided now was a good time for a compliment. "I know I value the chance to work for such an exciting new company."

His boss swallowed and looked down at his desk. "Exciting. New. Yes, those adjectives apply to us. Which can be both good and bad. For one, I know I haven't been able to pay you the salary someone with your talent deserves."

Teague wished he could figure out if Will was about to offer him a bonus or raise or promotion. Yet his terse expression and unwillingness to look him in the eyes indicated he had anything but good news. Maybe he needed reassurance Teague wasn't looking elsewhere for a better-paying job.

He decided to offer that assurance. "I might have landed a job at a more established place, but this company is a good thing. I like being able to bring my concerns directly to you, and I also appreciate that a smaller company can implement fewer rules and be more nimble than many larger firms. As I told you the day I accepted this job, I'm willing to take a little less in exchange for the opportunity to work here. In fact, I imagine your ears were burning the other night."

Will looked at him with interest. "Oh?"

"I was bragging about what a great boss you are and that you're letting me develop a Christian game. I think my date was impressed." Teague nodded and grinned. "So if you're wondering if I've changed my mind, I promise you I haven't."

"Oh." Will cleared his throat. "Thanks for the praise."

Teague became conscious of his breathing and the stillness that had entered the office without warning. From just outside the door, soft rock music was playing on a radio station that specialized in providing workplace tunes during the day.

Teague tapped his foot to the beat, more as a nervous response than enjoyment. He studied his boss's expression. Why was disappointment written on Will's face? Teague felt his body tense.

"I'd like to say that's great," Will continued, "but in this case I wish you did have job offers from other companies."

"You—you do?" Teague's stomach felt as though he were on a carnival ride right after eating a bag of popcorn and a funnel cake and slurping down a tall glass of soda. Unwilling to think through what his boss was trying to say, Teague remained silent and waited for him to spell out what he meant.

Will cleared his throat again and crossed his arms. "I think you are aware the Glasgow contract has always been iffy for us."

That was Teague's project. "Uh, I'm afraid so. You've been honest with me about that, and I appreciate it."

"They were wavering, and no matter how much I tried, I couldn't get the CEO behind us a hundred percent," Will said.

"But I thought the VP was happy with my work," Teague pointed out.

"He is. That's why they're paying us for what you've already done."

What he'd already done?

"Unfortunately," Will continued, "they have decided to cut the number of software titles they'll be releasing next year, so they terminated our contract."

"Cut the number of titles?" Teague repeated. "How did that happen?"

"They couldn't find adequate funds in their advertising budget to support it," Will explained. "You'll have to admit, a Christian title was a long shot for them."

"But I thought we had some support in marketing."

"We did, until they crunched the final numbers and they didn't add up the way they wanted them to. They decided to go with another company's idea instead." Will set his elbows on his desk and leaned toward Teague. "If you want my opinion, I think they decided they could generate more revenue with a street crime game."

Teague groaned. "I didn't go into this field to write games with violence and smut."

"And I wouldn't ask you to."

Teague had a thought. "But even if they can't use the games for personal computers, I thought they had plans to release a new game console. Can't they use it for that? Surely the market is broader there."

"I'm afraid not." Will shook his head. "Their marketing department didn't like the numbers their accountants came up with for the game console system either, so they decided to nix that, too."

"Looks like someone else will be getting bad news soon, too, then. That doesn't make me feel any better."

"Me either. Take a look at this. You'll be pleased with what they have to say about you." Will picked up a business letter printed on thick gray rag paper from the top of his desk and handed it to Teague.

He read it over, although the meaning of the letter barely registered in his mind. The letter was signed by his only ally at the company, the vice president, who had used the adjectives "imaginative," "character-building," "highly creative" and "stunning graphics" to describe the game Teague was developing. The praise was small comfort. How could he compliment Teague's work so highly in the first paragraph, only to ax the program in the second?

"I'm really sorry," was all Teague could say as he returned the letter to Will. "I was so sure that if I did my job well we could hold on to their business."

"Don't question yourself for a moment. The numbers were what made their decision for them. If you want to know my opinion, I'm likely to think they wouldn't have stayed with us this long if not for you and your work."

Teague sighed but mentally rolled up his sleeves in anticipation of a new course of action. "So do you want me to scrap this program or rework it?"

Will shook his head as he stared at the letter in his hands. "Neither."

"Neither?" The answer wasn't appealing. Teague knew he didn't want to get stuck with a dog of a contract. He had to speak up then and there to stake out a claim on another project. He ran down a mental list of the company's contracts. "I can help Justin with the new game he's developing if you like."

"Thanks, but he's got that under control."

"The BoomTown project then."

Will shook his head. "That's too close to a wrap for you to jump in now."

Teague took in a breath then swallowed. "I can help debug the calendar."

"I have Mary on that one."

A sense of desperation filled Teague. If he couldn't help on any of those projects, then what? He looked to his supervisor for a clue.

Will shook his head. "Believe me, I've tried to figure out where to plug you in here now that this contract has gone by the wayside, but I've got everyone working at optimum level now. If I were confident we'd be getting another new contract suited to your skills soon, I'd float you for a while. But because we're such a small company, I can't afford to keep you here indefinitely while we wait for the next contract."

Teague felt his chest tighten in fear. "You—you have no idea when that might happen?"

"I asked sales. Could be months." Frowning, he tossed the letter onto his desk. "I hate this about owning my own business. If I went public, I'd have more money to float me in situations like this, but my hands are tied."

"I understand." Teague wished he didn't. He wished he had some recourse, but he didn't see one. Even if he insisted on staying, how could he compel his boss to pay him money he didn't have? He supposed if the situation were reversed, Teague would be forced to make the same decision.

"I'm sorry," Will said.

"I know. And I understand," Teague assured him. "I'll go pack up my desk."

"No, don't do that yet. Stay until Friday so you can tie up the loose ends to close out the contract. I can pay you two weeks' salary as severance."

Two weeks' salary. Not much. "Thanks."

"I wish I could be more generous, and I wish it didn't have to be this way. If I could find a way to keep you, I would," Will told him. "Just know that once you start looking for a new job, send your prospective employers to me. I'll give you a glowing reference."

"I appreciate that." Teague tried not to slump his shoulders as he left the office. He knew the current economy meant that most people could expect to go from job to job in a heartbeat. He just didn't think he'd be laid off if he worked hard enough and showed his company unflagging dedication.

As he made his way back to his desk, Teague avoided making eye contact with any of his coworkers. He couldn't face them with the news. Not yet. He couldn't face anyone. He had no idea what he would do next.

&

That night Teague agonized over his job loss. Still too depressed to talk to anyone, he opted to stay home alone and sit in front of his computer. Scanning the Internet for job leads made him feel as though he were making an effort to improve his situation. With only two weeks' severance pay, finances were too tight to contemplate. He didn't want to think about how he would meet the next month's bills.

Discouraged, he thought about picking up the phone to call his father for a few encouraging words but thought better of it. His parents had supported him emotionally and financially as much as they could through school, and the last thing he wanted to do was ask for more money now. He ran down his list of financial obligations: rent, phone, food, utilities, gasoline, student loans, and car payment. Not much fluff. He had to find a new job soon.

He rummaged through the stack of papers on his small particleboard desk to see if he'd missed anything. The notice for the ski trip was near the top. Maybe he should cancel it. He'd get a few dollars back, and he also wouldn't have to worry about Kassia.

He kept reading. Too bad the deadline had passed for him to get either his or Kassia's deposits back. He sighed and searched for the most optimistic way to view his situation. Maybe skiing would get his mind off his troubles. Yes, that was it. That was the only way to look at his otherwise grim situation. Too bad the thought did little to cheer him.

A picture of Kassia popped into his head. The idea of being with her was still appealing, though. Maybe he wasn't sorry the deadline had passed.

five

The following weekend Kassia wiped down the kitchen counter even though it was already clean and she was dressed to go skiing. She had to do something to alleviate the tension she felt as she waited for Teague to arrive. She almost wished she'd agreed to meet him at the church instead. On second thought, no. Waiting at home was easier than being among a group of strangers.

What was she thinking when she accepted Teague's impromptu invitation? Well, at least she should be safe among those teens and the other chaperones. Even if Teague, like all the other men she had met, proved to be a wolf in sheep's clothing, most likely he valued his position as a youth leader too much to make a fool of himself chasing her around the ski lodge.

Now why would she think Teague would pursue her as more than a friend? Was that just ego talking? Then a picture of Brad popped into her mind. At that moment she realized she had allowed Brad's persistence to color her perceptions of Teague.

A few minutes later when her phone rang, Kassia was sure the caller would be Teague saying he was on his way to pick her up or he'd be late. Instead a familiar female voice spoke.

"Lexie!" Kassia squealed into the phone. "You've been so scarce lately."

"I know, and I'm sorry. I've been meaning to call, but you know how it is."

Kassia swallowed. She wished she did know what it was like to be a newlywed and to be as content as Lexie obviously was with Theo. Would she ever find such happiness for herself?

"I can only imagine how busy you are." Knowing Lexie, they'd be talking for a while. Kassia sat on the couch and leaned back against the cushions. "How was your trip? You went to the Bahamas, didn't you?"

"Our trip was as wonderful as any honeymoon could be!" Lexie cooed into the phone. "Yes, we did go to a resort in the Bahamas. It was fantastic."

"I'm sure! Did the weather hold out for you?"

"Yes! The sun was wonderful."

"So you had quite a bit of beach time." Kassia thought it was funny she was talking about the beach when she was about to go skiing in the mountains.

"Every day. I managed to get a good tan. You should have seen the water, Kassia. It's a transparent blue-green I've never seen anywhere else. And the sand is so white."

"Sounds beautiful. Did you go scuba diving like you hoped to?"

"We sure did. We rented an underwater camera so we can bore everybody to death with our pictures of underwater life."

Kassia laughed. "I'd like to see those sometime. But as exciting as staying underwater sounds, I think I'd rather have spent my time in the city."

"I don't know if you'd call Nassau a city like the ones you're used to. It's charming but not too big. We took a shuttle into the town then went for a carriage ride around the city and saw the governor's mansion," Lexie said. "They drive on the left side of the road there, which was different for me."

"Did you go shopping and get any good deals?"

"I didn't buy much. They had a surprising number of street vendors. I think they get a lot of business because so many cruise ships dock there."

"Makes sense," Kassia agreed.

"Quite a few little children were selling trinkets, and some offered to braid hair."

"I'll bet they were sweet. Who can turn down a little kid?" Kassia remarked.

"You're so right. As you can imagine, I came back with a braid in my hair. Those kids made me miss Piper even more than I thought possible."

"So you bought her a bunch of trinkets?"

"I managed to control myself for the most part." Lexie chuckled. "I did get a little handmade doll for Piper from a woman selling them on the street. The doll had a hat and skirt woven out of straw. The woman sewed her name right into the skirt while we waited."

"Wow! I'd call that good service." Kassia smiled. "I'm sure Piper liked that. And I'm sure she missed you as much as you missed her."

"I don't know about that. Maybe a little bit. She was having fun at her grandma's." Kassia heard Lexie sigh. "Now it's back to reality for all of us."

"But your reality isn't so bad, is it?"

"Not at all. But it's a lot more like a rat race here in the States, running Piper to day care, running to work, running back to pick her up, running home to fix supper," Lexie said. "The pace of life is so much slower there. No one is in a hurry to do anything. At least that's the way it seemed to me."

"Sounds like fun for a few weeks, but I'm not sure I'd like to live at such a slow pace all the time," Kassia said.

"Hmm. Maybe not," Lexie agreed. "I am glad to be back home. Or should I say, Theo's house?"

"It's your house now, too," Kassia reminded her.

"I know. It's hard to think of it as mine, though. I'm looking around now and thinking how difficult that is to believe."

Kassia remembered how Theo had barely touched his new house to decorate it. The last time she visited, the walls were bare except for a few framed posters. The furniture consisted of a few pieces from the off-campus apartment he rented during college, and they were hardly heirloom quality. She could just imagine how nice the house would look after Lexie had a hand in beautifying it. "You'll put your own touches on it soon enough, and then you won't remember a time when it didn't feel like your own. I'm sure you've already thought about decorating, haven't you?"

"You know me too well. I've already consulted an interior decorator for the family room and dining room since more people will be seeing those than some of the other rooms—like Theo's office. That's hopeless!" She chuckled.

"Aren't most home offices?" Kassia pointed out.

"Probably," Lexie admitted. "I don't blame Theo for wanting at least one room to keep as his own private space. After all, Piper and I have descended upon him with all our girlie-girl possessions."

Kassia smiled and twisted the phone cord. "I'm sure he loves every minute of it."

"He seems to. I'm so grateful he and Piper are still getting along well. He took care of her the other night while I met with the decorator. I want to get drapes and wallpaper to match. Maybe in blue."

"You'll be busy, but I'm sure Theo will like the results. I know that place needs some color. Does Piper like her room?"

"She does. I'm letting her choose the color she wants it painted. So far she's picked out several shades of pink."

"Good for her."

"Oh, by the way, Theo and I are enjoying the espresso machine you gave us. It looks great in our kitchen."

"Good." Kassia had splurged on their wedding gift. Lexie had once mentioned how much she missed having home-brewed espresso coffee since leaving North Carolina. "I'm glad I was able to get you something you wanted."

"Now I feel like I'm at home when I use your gift. And I want you to come for a visit soon and try a cup for yourself. You don't have to wait for the drapes to arrive."

"I will. Visit soon, that is." Kassia could imagine Lexie, content in her own kitchen, making breakfast for Theo and Piper.

"You're living a fairy tale. After all this time, you deserve it."

"Thanks, but I'm no more worthy than anyone else. I'm just thankful the Lord has chosen to bless me far beyond what I imagined. But since you brought up the subject of fairy tales, I understand you might be in the process of creating a story of your own," Lexie noted.

"Me? What do you mean?"

"Don't try to fool me. I know all about how well you and Teague hit it off at our wedding."

"And how do you know that?" Kassia twisted the phone cord even more tightly around her fingers. She could feel her pulse picking up speed.

"Teague told Theo, of course."

"I might have known. And they say we girls are the ones who do all the gossiping." Kassia smiled.

"I wouldn't call it gossiping."

"Well, maybe not," Kassia conceded.

"Theo is just happy things are going so well for you two."

"So far, so good."

"I told you I was going to set you up with a great guy. Wasn't I right?"

"Yeah, he's pretty nice."

"So tell me everything!"

"We went out to dinner, and now we have a date to go skiing, if that tells you anything," Kassia said.

"Skiing? Wow! You move fast."

"I'm waiting for him to pick me up now, as a matter of fact."

"Oh, then I'd better hang up," Lexie said.

"No need to yet. Talking to you is making the time go by much faster," Kassia said. "But, you know, I think he asked me more out of spontaneity than anything else. We're going with his church youth group."

Lexie chuckled. "Then he's recruited you to go on a working vacation."

"That's what it sounds like, but I don't think he expects me to do much in the way of watching the teens. Anyway, I imagine they're old enough to take care of themselves."

"Maybe that's not such a good thing."

"Hmm. I hadn't thought of it that way. Well, I'm sure Teague knows what to do. And there are supposed to be some other chaperones." Kassia took a fork in the conversational road. "Speaking of teen youth groups, I might have known you'd try to match me up with someone who goes to church all the time."

"Oh, Kassia, we didn't put you two together as a ploy to get you to church. I don't believe the Lord would want anyone to force Him on them," Lexie explained. "Theo and I just thought you and Teague would enjoy each other while you were at the wedding. We weren't trying to create any attachment beyond that. I promise. But judging from the fact you're still seeing each other, it looks like our instincts guided us well."

"That remains to be seen," Kassia said. "I do have a question for you. Is Teague sincere about his faith?"

"Of course he is," Lexie said quickly. "He's one of the most devout Christians I know." Her voice held a note of triumph, as though she was certain Kassia would be pleased to make such a discovery. "Why do you ask? Doesn't he seem sincere to you?"

Rather than comforting Kassia, Lexie's assessment only made her more anxious. At least she was used to wolves. She hadn't been that close to men from church in a long time.

"Sure he seems sincere," Kassia told Lexie. "I just wanted to know. Some men can be good actors, you know." She heard Teague's knock on the door. "Speaking of men, here is our devout Christian now. Gotta go."

"Have fun!" Lexie said before hanging up the phone.

"I will. I hope," Kassia muttered to herself after putting the phone down.

She threw open the door to find Teague with a self-assured expression, dressed in a sharp-looking blue-and-white ski bib. He looked much more confident than Kassia felt.

"I hate to rush you," he said, "but I guess you figured out I'm running late. I'm sorry about that."

"No problem," she assured him. "I doubt they can leave before you get there anyway."

"Yeah, that's one of the perks of being the leader." He looked at his watch. "But there's late, and then there's really late. And if we don't hurry, we'll be really late."

Teague was gentleman enough to pick up Kassia's suitcase that was sitting by the door. The small gesture made her feel pampered.

They exited her apartment amid laughter. For the first time since she'd last seen Teague, Kassia felt her heart was as bright as the sun shining over the horizon.

Later, on the way to the ski resort, Kassia felt self-conscious. The church van proclaimed HIS KINGDOM AND HOLINESS CHURCH in bright red letters on each side, followed by their city and a phone number. If that wasn't enough, the phrase JESUS IS LORD OF ALL was painted in bold orange letters on the front and back of the fifteen-passenger vehicle. She knew everyone passing them on the road would stare.

Once she'd been in the van awhile, she realized she wasn't used to being around teens. They had brought music tapes along for the ride, so the stereo blasted Christian tunes she barely knew. The whole scene made her feel uncomfortable at first. At least they didn't tease her about being with Teague, unlike his predictions. That is, they didn't tease her to her face.

Three hours later they pulled into the driveway of a ski lodge that reminded her of pictures she'd seen of wooden Swiss chalets. The roof was covered with snow, and streams of smoke proceeded from both chimneys. The cold wind hit her face rudely as soon as they disembarked from the snug van. Kassia was eager to get in the lodge so she could sit by the fire with a cup of cocoa.

"You'll be at the meeting, won't you?" Teague asked as the group unloaded their suitcases from the van, chattered, and stretched their legs.

"Uh, meeting? What meeting?"

"Oh, I didn't tell you before?" His mouth set in a chagrined line. "It's nothing formal. After we check in, we'll be meeting by the back fireplace for a little fellowship along with a bit of praise and worship music." He tilted his head toward one of the teens. "Matt brought his guitar. It'll be fun."

"Yeah." Kassia squirmed. Why did they have to spoil the whole ski trip by demanding that everyone attend a hymn sing-along?

"You like music, don't you?" His voice was encouraging.

"Yeah, I guess." She would never admit she was rusty on singing hymns. Even after several hours of listening to Christian music in the van, she was sure she wouldn't know any of the contemporary tunes the teens preferred.

Teague picked up his green nylon suitcase with one hand and retrieved Kassia's red bag with the other.

"You don't have to carry that." She reached out to grab her bag.

"I don't mind." He started walking up the stone pathway that had been cleared of snow. Kassia strode by his side to keep the pace. "No one expects you to know the songs by heart," Teague assured her. "You can just listen to the words and maybe learn them that way, if you like." He sent her a disarming grin. "Why not come along and bring your Bible?"

"I thought it was just going to be music."

"And a little bit of study and reading. Nothing long. I promise no one will ask hard questions or put you on the spot."

She nodded toward the other chaperones, who she gathered were parents of some of the kids. "Are you sure? They might ask a hard question."

"Leslie and Marvin?" He shook his head. "They won't bother you. They're not here to judge. Besides, they leave the teaching to me."

"Then I know I'm in trouble." She laughed at her own joke, but Kassia felt the heat spreading over her face. She held open the door for Teague to enter the lodge. "Um, I didn't realize we needed our Bibles. I left mine at home."

"Not a problem." He grinned at her again. "I'll share mine with you."

Following him to the reception desk, she wished she could come up with some other reason why she couldn't attend, but no convincing reason—at least none she wanted to share with Teague—came to mind. How could he know her memories of the church youth group she once despised when she was a teenager? She had been different from the others and had felt excluded. Her parents' prestigious positions didn't matter to her peers, so their acceptance wasn't a given. Besides, the leaders rammed the Bible down her throat and made her feel like an unredeemable sinner.

Seeing no other alternative, she swallowed the lump in her throat. "Uh, that would be nice. Thanks."

"The meeting will be short since everyone will want to eat soon."

She nodded. At least God had some mercy after all.

After an easy check-in, Kassia hurried to her room to change into a pair of fresh indigo jeans and a soft white turtleneck sweater. Feeling confident after freshening up, she ventured down the rustic but sturdy wooden stairs to face the whole group.

Lord, please don't let me make a fool of myself.

She took in a breath and stopped in her tracks. "Did I just pray?" When was the last time she'd said a little prayer, a casual request thrown skyward as though He were listening? She shuddered. Teague was getting to her after all. She couldn't let him know. At least not yet.

six

Teague's face lit up a few moments later when he saw Kassia looking in the direction of the stone fireplace in the far corner of the lobby. "Over here." He motioned with a sweep of his hand for her to join the youth group, which was just getting ready to begin their time of fellowship.

Teague positioned himself on a comfortable-looking brown couch and leaned his elbow on the armrest. Kassia decided to sit beside him but made sure she wasn't close enough to touch him. He looked pleased by her selection of where to sit.

She set a Bible on her lap.

"I see we won't have to share after all," Teague remarked, disappointment shading his voice.

"I'm thankful for the Gideons. They're always so super about placing Bibles in hotel dresser drawers, aren't they?"

Teague nodded. "That's a great ministry. I wonder how many people have been saved because of those Bibles."

"Maybe we can write them and ask sometime."

Teague was nodding when a petite brunette teen interrupted with a question for him.

The singing hadn't started yet, and no one else paid Kassia any notice—another reason to give thanks. She was also glad she hadn't told Teague she could strum a few chords on her acoustic guitar. Otherwise, he might have asked her to bring it and play along with Matt. Then how would she look to everyone when they discovered she knew very few Christian songs?

Looking around the room, she realized the teens had split off into groups and pairs. Sitting on various seats that matched the couch where she sat with Teague, on the floor, or on the edge of the coffee table, they chattered among themselves as though they hadn't seen each other in years despite the fact they had just shared a long van ride.

Since Teague was still in the midst of conversation with several teens, Kassia made herself content to watch the flames crackling in the fireplace, offering a cozy feeling to the area. The fire accomplished no small feat considering the ceiling, unpainted and with beams exposed, was at least fifteen feet above the knotty pine floor.

Soon Teague rose to his feet and summoned everyone to attention so the meeting could start. A few other guests lingered nearby, but he didn't seem the least bit self-conscious as he led the group in an opening prayer. Peeking from half-open eyes, Kassia noticed that one couple looked up from reading their books, but otherwise no one expressed any surprise by their action. Teague sent up praises to the Lord, thanked Him for a safe journey and for their time together then prayed for various people who were having difficulties in their church. When he paused, a couple of members of the group mentioned some other names and prayed. When the petitions were exhausted, Teague ended with the group saying the Lord's Prayer in unison. Kassia had no problem reciting the prayer, a part of church life she had not forgotten.

Opening her eyes, Kassia felt moved by how the group genuinely cared about church members who were suffering. Their prayers brought back memories of how her own church had cared for its members. Often her mother would take meals to sick or grieving people and gifts to new parents. To her surprise Kassia missed knowing she was part of a congregation, a group of people she could depend on in her joys and sorrows.

Before she could meditate any further, Matt took charge of the meeting and led them in singing "Amazing Grace." The words came back to her as easily as if she had sung them the previous day. Maybe she could feel comfortable in the group after all.

"Okay, everyone," Teague said after thanking Matt for providing the tune, "who remembers our scripture verse for the week?"

Several hands shot up, and as many voices said more or less in unison, " 'With God all things are possible'—Matthew 19:26!"

Kassia nearly jumped at the volume of their response. She hadn't seen a group of teens seem so excited or eager to show they remembered a verse. Slightly embarrassed, she glanced at a few other guests who were within hearing range. One couple who looked to be over thirty smiled at their enthusiasm. A group of younger guys appeared to be as amazed as Kassia.

"Good job!" Teague beamed. "And who said this?"

"Jesus!" answered several voices.

"Can anyone tell me why He said this?"

This question brought a slight pause. Kassia searched her mind until she thought she remembered the answer but, recalling her earlier prayer, decided not to risk making a fool of herself.

"Remember?" Teague prodded. "We went into this a little bit last week. Didn't any of you go home and read the verses for yourself?"

Most of the teens looked at the floor, apparently to avoid eye contact with their leader, and the room grew quiet.

Finally someone answered.

"Because," a boy said from the back, "He had just said it's easier for a camel to walk through the eye of a needle than it is for a rich man to enter the kingdom of God."

"Right. Good job, Rick. I'm glad to see someone is doing his homework." Teague's voice held enough reprimand in it to show he was disappointed.

"So was there an actual gate named 'Eye of the Needle'?" Matt asked.

"That's a good question," Teague answered. "What do you think?"

"I don't know. That's why I asked you."

Kassia laughed along with the others.

"I don't think there was such a gate," another young man said. "I think that's just a theory somebody made up to explain something they didn't understand."

"There might have been," one teen disagreed. "I don't think you can prove there wasn't."

After several rounds of banter and exchange of opinions, someone returned to the central issue. "So it's impossible for a rich man to enter heaven?"

"Well," Teague said, "what does our verse of the week say about that?"

"That everything is possible with God," a few answered.

"Oh yeah." The questioner blushed several shades of crimson while his friends nearby poked him in the ribs and teased him for not listening earlier.

"You know, I heard most people have to hear something eight times before it sinks in," Teague said. "So all good verses bear repeating."

"Or maybe fifteen times in some cases," one of the girls said amid chortles and snickers.

"Okay, guys. You've had your fun. Now, Ariana." He nodded toward a girl sitting on the floor by the coffee table. "What verse do you think we should memorize while we're on the slopes?"

"It's funny you should say that," Ariana responded. "I found a verse I like about a mountain." She opened her Bible. "Mark 11:23."

Kassia remembered Mark as being located in the New Testament, but she wasn't quick to find the right place. She couldn't help but notice that Teague flipped without effort to the passage.

"Everybody got it?" he asked soon after pages stopped rustling. After receiving nods and affirmative answers, Teague indicated Ariana could begin reading.

" 'I tell you the truth, if anyone says to this mountain, "Go, throw yourself into the sea," and does not doubt in his heart but believes that what he says will happen, it will be done for him.' "

"So how many mountains are you going to move tomorrow, Ariana?" Teague asked, smiling.

"Not too many, I hope." Ariana, a pert young woman with sandy blond hair, laughed.

Kassia chuckled along with the rest of the crowd. She enjoyed being part of the group. She had never seen such a relaxed atmosphere and easy camaraderie in what amounted to a Sunday school class. Clearly these kids were friends with each other and didn't mind sharing their foibles as they talked about the Bible. She hadn't heard a word of Christian jargon. Anyone, even someone of a different faith altogether, would have no trouble understanding what both Teague and his youth group said. The teens seemed interested, too, in what he had to say. Kassia didn't see any bored faces or irreverent expressions on their faces.

They were as respectful of one another when different members of the group spoke. Each person seemed to listen to the others' ideas. No one tried to outdo anyone else or embarrass those who weren't well versed. Kassia liked how Teague emphasized the positive aspects of scripture. Talk of condemnation was absent. Yet Kassia sensed that most of the students realized scripture wasn't all sweetness and love. Some posed hard questions to Teague about faith, and she found herself impressed by his answers.

Even more surprising, Kassia didn't look at her watch once during the lesson. Before she knew the time was up, Teague called for a round of songs to close. Distressed when she realized the tune was unfamiliar, Kassia mouthed the words at first, although she soon caught on to the verses as they repeated the chorus several times. The uplifting words about God's love left her feeling ready to face whatever challenges the slopes—and life—had to offer.

"So what did you think?" Teague asked her after the meeting.

She nodded. "I liked it. It was nice not to be taken on a guilt trip."

"If I took you on a guilt trip, I'd have to ride in the front seat right along with you," Teague confessed. "In fact everyone here would."

She eyed Ariana and Matt. "Your whole group seems as if they know it."

"I try to keep them humble." He chuckled. "Seriously, I always caution everyone that if we correct our brothers and sisters in Christ, we must approach them not as perfect people but as genuinely flawed also. We're all on this journey here together. No one but the Lord got through without making a mistake."

"I know. And it's nice to hear a Christian teacher admit that for a change."

A few moments later, they sat down to a meal of spaghetti in a large room filled with long tables. Kassia let the chatter of the group flow over and around her as she became lost in her own thoughts. Maybe God did want her to come back to the church after her lapse during college. Maybe He could get her back on track. She prayed He could—and would.

Kassia recalled the verse she had forgotten from her youth, the one the group had talked about earlier. *"With God all things are possible."*

Even for a rich man to enter the kingdom of heaven. Even for Kassia Dahl to experience His good grace.

The hours passed much faster than Kassia could have imagined the previous week. As far as she knew, no one tried to move any mountains; but she felt her faith reawakened and grow as she enjoyed the fellowship of the group and marveled at the beauty of the Lord's creation. She hadn't been skiing in years, but she found her skill level increasing as the days flew by. Later in the trip, she even found the nerve to try an intermediate run. Her only disappointment came because Teague was responsible for the kids, so his time with her was limited. Yet considering the fact they were hardly what anyone could call a couple, and Teague hadn't asked her to help teach or chaperone, she knew she had no right to complain. At least she could sit beside him during the meals. She ate heartily after a day of exercise in the frigid weather.

As the trip progressed, a few of the teens discovered Teague had invited Kassia. As he had predicted, they had to counter the occasional good-natured ribbing. Kassia discovered she didn't mind being associated with Teague. To her delight, she noticed only a hint of embarrassment was evident underneath his responsive grin. Maybe he didn't mind they were considered a twosome either. The thought didn't displease her.

"Do you think the girls are disappointed now that some of the group has decided to link us together?" Kassia asked half jokingly when they were out of earshot one evening.

Teague's eyebrows shot up, and his mouth formed a circle. "You're kidding, right?"

"Only a little."

"They think I'm an old man," he answered. "And sometimes I think they're right." He rubbed his thigh. "Only an old guy would ache this much after skiing."

He reminded Kassia of her own sore muscles. She covered her upper and lower front teeth with her lips. "Then I—I must be pretty old t—too," she said, her voice shaking, " 'cause my old muscles are g—giving me a fit. M—maybe, dearie, we should try one of those n—newfangled aspirin tablets. I—I heard they're the l—latest miracle drug."

Teague laughed at her antics. "Yep, they work mightily."

Kassia marveled at how comfortable she had become with Teague, a man who had made her somewhat fearful only a short while before. But at the same time she was thankful she felt so accepted by him—and his group.

Even more surprising, she began to look forward to the time of fellowship, teaching, and praise after a full day of skiing. Teague's knowledge of the Bible was evident in his lessons. Kassia admired the way he allowed the kids to introduce questions. Never did he condemn them or question their level of commitment. She realized he treated her with the same respect. Perhaps his respect was the reason she didn't run away from him or the group, despite being expected to participate in the lessons. When Teague suggested further reading, no one was more surprised than Kassia when she wrote down the passages and resolved to read them.

The last day of the trip came all too soon. Kassia awoke to sunlight streaming in through the window and the sound of her two young roommates snoring in the adjacent bed. Since they had shared the room together, Ariana and Emily had taken the liberty of asking how she knew Teague. Once she explained they were friends who met at a wedding, the girls let the subject drop. Kassia was thankful they didn't ask more. She didn't know how she would have answered more probing queries.

"Time to get up if you two want to get any more skiing in before we leave." Kassia shook the lump under the covers that was nearest to her. "We can only ski until noon."

One of the girls groaned. "Just until noon?"

"Yes. That's what Teague said."

"Umm."

She shook the sleeping form again. "Come on. Up and at 'em."

"I don't wanna get up," Emily moaned.

"How about you, Ariana?"

Kassia's question was met with another groan.

"All right then. If you want to sleep until noon instead of skiing, it's not my fault. Don't say I didn't try to get you out of bed." Kassia suspected both girls, who were expert skiers, would appear downstairs for breakfast in a matter of minutes.

By the time she checked out and left her suitcases with everyone else's from the group, Kassia had enough time to grab a muffin and a cup of hot cocoa to fortify herself before she took one or two more runs on the slopes. She looked around the dining hall for Teague, hoping that perhaps they could spend a few moments together before they had to share their company with the others. Then she searched the lobby. He was nowhere to be found in the lodge. Kassia speculated for an instant that maybe he had remained in bed to catch up on lost sleep. Just as quickly, the thought popped out of her head. Teague would find it impossible to oversleep. By being the first to hit the slopes each day, he had proven himself to be a true morning person.

She spent her last morning in a state of halfway happiness as she skied with various members of the group. Finally Teague caught up with her just before noon as she was planning to make one last run.

"Looks as if you survived," Teague greeted her. Hot breath met with chilly air, forming a mist of steam with each word. Despite the sun's position high in the sky, its rays seemed to do little to warm the earth.

"So far, so good. Where were you?" she couldn't resist asking.

"I tried out the expert slope."

"Oh, that explains why I couldn't find you. How was it?"

"Great!" She could see the outline of a broad smile underneath his blue knitted ski mask.

"What made you decide to come back to the easy slope?"

"Maybe I wanted to find you." Teague looked at his watch.

"We have time for one last run before we have to go."

"That's what I thought. I had planned on making this one my last."

"You've gotten pretty good at skiing over the weekend. I'm surprised you didn't try the expert run at least once before we left."

"I may have gotten good, but not that good. Or that daring." She shuddered at the thought of injuring herself but recovered long enough to wish him well. "Make it a good one!" she shouted.

"I will!" He pushed off and started down the run.

Kassia watched Teague head down the hill, mentally applauding his smooth style and expert movements. She smiled. Then, without warning, Kassia heard a snapping sound.

Teague's right ski shot upward. He swayed to one side, skiing on one foot to maintain his position on both legs.

She gasped. Had Teague struck some object hidden under the snow?

Where is he going?

She watched as he veered off course and headed toward a cluster of pine trees.

"Watch out, Teague!" she screamed, even though she knew he couldn't hear her. "Watch out!"

Her warnings were in vain. In horror, she watched Teague collide into a tree.

"Teague! No!"

seven

Kassia skied as fast as she could to where Teague lay on the ground. She stopped and knelt beside him in her skis and examined his still form. His eyes were closed. She took off her glove and placed her hand under his nose. She felt hot breaths against her skin.

Kassia glanced up at the cloudless blue sky. "Thank You, Lord." She didn't care who heard her prayer of gratitude.

Gently she slapped both sides of his face. "Teague! Teague! It's me! Wake up!" She quivered with fear.

She was so absorbed in trying to wake Teague that she barely heard the swishing of snow behind her. She turned only when a shadow blocked the sun's rays.

"Don't do anything else, ma'am."

She looked up and saw a figure dressed in black ski garb with a patch bearing the words "Ski Patrol" on it. A second man in a similar outfit stopped just behind him.

Good! They'll help him!

"Let us take it from here." The first patrolman crouched down near Teague's prone form.

"Is he going to be all right?" As she stepped aside to make room for the patrolman, panic registered in her voice.

From the corner of her eye, she noticed the second patrolman directing other skiers away from the scene. The top of the hill, where skiers had been lined up waiting for their turns only moments before, was now deserted. No voices carried through the chilled air. No one raced down the slope. The silence seemed eerie.

"There's nothing for you to worry about, ma'am. We're

doing everything we can. I've already called for assistance. But right now we need to examine him." The patrolman's tone was firm but gentle. "Did you see how this happened?"

Kassia nodded. "Yes, I did. He had just pushed off and was heading downhill when it looked like his ski hit something in the path and threw him off course. He tried to regain his balance, but he lost control and ran into these trees."

"So he wasn't moving too fast then."

"No. He hadn't had time to build up much speed."

"That's lucky."

Kassia shuddered. She knew the patrolman had left some words unspoken. Images of Teague sustaining far greater injuries—or even death—entered her mind. She shook her head, forcing such horrible images to exit.

"The funny thing is," she explained, "he's a good skier. He had been on the tougher slopes and was making this easier one his last run." Kassia realized she was offering more information than was necessary or even interesting to someone assisting Teague with his injuries. Yet for some reason she wanted the patrolmen to know Teague was accomplished in the sport.

"Thank you, ma'am. You've helped us a lot. Now the best thing you can do at the moment is to move aside and let us do our work." Despite his command his voice was gentle. He studied her for an instant. "Are you his wife?"

The patrolman's words left a knot in her stomach. Suddenly she wished she could claim the privilege. "No. He's not married."

"Is there a responsible party that can be reached?"

"We're with a church group. Someone will make sure his family is told there was an accident." Kassia hovered a few feet away as the patrolmen examined Teague.

She watched and waited. Now that she was no longer moving, she became conscious of the cold. Even worse, she felt helpless. If only she could do something, anything, to help!

"Is he going to be all right?" she asked when they started mumbling to each other in sounds she couldn't discern.

"We'll know more after he's been checked out thoroughly at the hospital."

"The hospital?" As soon as she blurted out the words, she knew how silly she must have sounded. Teague was unconscious. Of course he would have to go to the hospital.

At that moment a paramedic appeared on a snow cat. The sight made her feel more fearful but at the same time relieved. "Where are they taking him?"

"To the lodge so the regular ambulance can take him to the nearest hospital."

A mental picture of Teague lying prone and helpless in a hospital bed upset her even more.

The paramedic knelt beside Teague and gave him a quick examination of his own. "It looks as if he did some damage to his right ankle," Kassia heard him mutter to a patrolman. "It's already swollen to double the size it should be."

"How about the other one?"

With a gentle motion he lifted Teague's other ankle. "It appears to be okay."

She let out her breath then watched him look over the new patient. Moments later Kassia heard the verdict. "He's got a nasty bump on his head, but I don't see any other evidence of broken bones."

Broken bones!

"All right. He's ready to go," he said.

Kassia cringed but gathered enough courage to speak. "I want to go with him."

"You said you aren't his wife," the patrolman standing near her said. "Are you any relation to him?"

"No, but neither is anyone else here. He needs someone to be with him. He shouldn't be alone." She tried to speak calmly but could hear her voice rising.

The patrolmen exchanged looks; then the one who had been friendly to Kassia nodded. "Okay. You can ride along to the hospital."

"Thank you!"

A short time later, they were almost to the lodge when Kassia spotted one of the church chaperones, Marvin, and hurried to him.

Marvin glanced up as Kassia approached. "Oh no. Tell me that's not somebody from our group lying on that stretcher."

"I wish it wasn't, but it is." She blinked back tears that loomed in the corners of her eyes. "Teague had an accident."

"An accident? Will he be all right?" Marvin asked.

"I don't know. I don't know anything." Kassia still struggled to hold back tears. She couldn't break down now. She didn't want to appear frantic or scared. If she did anything that looked untoward, the patrolmen were certain to keep her from going to the hospital with Teague. "Why don't I stay with him?"

"You look upset," Marvin said. "Are you sure that's not too big of a burden for you?"

"No, of course not." Then the plight of the teens occurred to her. "But I feel bad about leaving the kids stranded. They have to get back home, and it doesn't look like Teague will be driving anytime soon. Can you make sure everyone gets home? Do you mind?"

He nodded. "Sure, I'll be glad to do that. I can drive the van. Not a problem."

Another thought occurred to her. "Do you know Teague's family?"

"Not well," he admitted, "but I've met them."

"I hate to ask, but do you mind calling them? Someone needs to know what's happened."

He nodded. "I hate being the bearer of bad news, but it

can't be helped. What do you think we should tell them? We don't know much yet."

"Just tell them the truth. That Teague is in the hospital. Tell them I'm going with him so they'll know he's not alone, okay?"

"Do they know you?"

She shifted uneasily. "No, they don't."

Surely before all was said and done, she would end up meeting them. If only their first encounter didn't have to occur under such harrowing circumstances.

But I wouldn't want to be anywhere else.

Another thought occurred to her. "Can you get my suitcase out of the van? I'm sure I'll be needing some clothes before all is said and done. And maybe you'd better get Teague's also."

"Sure thing." The older man hurried to the parking lot to complete his errand as the regular ambulance arrived.

Throughout the nerve-racking ride to the hospital along winding mountain roads with sharp hairpin turns, Kassia held on to Teague's hand as though his life—and hers—depended on her ability to maintain her grasp.

Once they pulled into the emergency room entrance at the hospital, she was moved out of the way, however politely. Feeling stranded, she found the nearby waiting room and took a seat. Most of the people she shared the room with were slouched in various chairs, looking as depressed and anxious as she felt.

Old television sets hung from braces in each upper corner of the room. They were tuned to different stations, with their volumes turned just high enough to be heard in the immediate area. She found no interest in soap operas showing the antics of overdressed actresses and perfectly groomed actors. A talk show featured disheveled people screaming at each other. Seeing no middle ground on television and no easy way to change the channels, Kassia grabbed several worn-out magazines and sat down in a blue vinyl chair in hopes of finding some articles of interest to pass the time.

Just when she thought she had read every magazine published in the past year, a middle-aged nurse, wearing a blue lab coat printed with cartoonish dogs, entered and asked if anyone was with Teague Boswell. Kassia nodded toward the nurse and rose from her seat.

"How is he?"

"Stable," she answered in a quiet but authoritative voice. She began walking down the corridor.

Kassia followed. "Stable. What does that mean? Is he awake?"

"He hasn't regained consciousness yet."

She felt a lump in her throat. "That's not good, is it?"

The nurse paused for a second. "It would be better for him to regain consciousness as soon as possible, but it's not time to worry yet." She smiled. "Doctor Kahn can tell you more. I'm sure he'll be in soon." The nurse stopped in front of a door. "Here he is."

Kassia peered in and noticed Teague's ankle was bandaged.

"His ankle broke in the fall, I'm afraid," the nurse explained, confirming what the paramedic had suspected. "I'm sure he'll need surgery. I'm sorry." The nurse gave Kassia a warm but professional smile. "I'm sure he'll be glad to see you when he wakes up. I'll be at the nurses' station if you need anything. It's just down the hall. Take the first left, and it's right there. Do you need me to show you?"

"No, that's okay. I'll be fine. Thanks." When Kassia went into the room, she was taken aback when she saw him lying in bed motionless and silent except for regular beeps from the machines attached to him. The still form was such a far cry from the lively man she knew. She drew in a breath and braced herself then approached the side of the bed until she was close enough to study his face. To her surprise he looked peaceful, as though he were having a pleasant dream and had no idea his life was in danger.

She stroked his forehead. "I hope you are having sweet dreams, Teague." If only she weren't so powerless. She wished she could help him. She wished she were lying in the bed, instead of him.

Strange. I've never felt that way about anyone before. How can I have such a depth of emotion about a man I don't know all that well yet?

She was glad she hadn't told her family much about this new man in her life, a man who had suddenly and unexpectedly taken on such importance to her. What would they think if they could see her now?

Her sisters would probably be amused by her intense response to Teague. They would call her flighty and say her impulsiveness was par for the course. Father would be supportive but caution her not to move too fast.

Mother's judgment would be the most difficult to bear. She would no doubt chastise Kassia for wanting to take Teague's place in the hospital bed. "If the Lord intended for you to be lying in that bed, He would have put you there." She could hear Mother's voice echoing in her thoughts.

Feeling like a misbehaving little girl, Kassia unzipped her neon yellow waist pack and withdrew her cell phone. She looked down at her clothes and suddenly realized she still hadn't changed her outfit.

I hope no one minds seeing me in ski clothes.

She dialed a number and waited through three rings.

Her mother's crisp voice answered. "Hello?"

"Mother?"

"Kassia? Is that you?"

"It's me," Kassia confirmed.

"Where are you? I've tried to reach you at home. Surely you aren't still on the ski trip? Don't you have to go back to work sometime? You can't expect them to let you take off the rest of the week just so you can ski." Her tone was sharp.

"Trust me, I'm not having fun out on the slopes. That ended before noon today. And don't worry about my work. I'll call in and let my boss know what happened."

"What happened? What do you mean?

Kassia reviewed the events of the day.

"Let me get this straight," her mother said. "You're there in the hospital with this Teague Boswell, a man you hardly know. A man I never even heard you mention until you were a bridesmaid in Lexie's wedding."

Kassia groaned. Her mother could make the most innocent event seem like international intrigue. "Mother, it's not like that. He's lying here unconscious."

"I'm sorry to hear that, but he's not your responsibility. Doesn't he have a family somewhere?"

"Yes, and I asked someone from his church to notify them. I'm sure they'll be here as soon as they can," Kassia said.

"How are you going to get home?"

In her excitement and distress, Kassia hadn't thought about being stranded at the hospital.

"How could you make such a blunder, Kassia?" her mother scolded. "Honestly, you never seem to think about the consequences of anything you do. You just run off on impulse and worry about how everything will turn out later. I wish you would be more careful when you make decisions."

"I'm sorry."

"Don't tell me you're sorry. Tell that to whoever has to be certain you get home safely."

"I'm sure I can ride back with someone from Teague's family," Kassia said. At least she hoped she could.

"I certainly hope so. How long will he be in the hospital?"

"I don't know. He broke his right ankle and will need surgery on that."

"Then he won't be able to drive a car until it heals. He'll be just as dependent on others as you are now." Her mother let out an exasperated sigh.

"Don't worry. Please. I'm sure someone will help me out. I can take care of it."

"It was foolish of you to put yourself in the position of relying on strangers." Mother sighed again. "Look—if you really need us to, I suppose we can come and pick you up."

The offer was tempting, but Kassia knew she would endure a lecture all the way home if she accepted. "Thanks, but I'll get home."

"I will pray for your friend to recover. I hope he wakes up."

Kassia hadn't considered the possibility that he might not wake up at all. "I'm sure he'll wake up soon." Her voice quivered in spite of her efforts to put up a calm front.

"I hope so. But once he does, he'll be laid up awhile with his ankle," Mother said.

"You're probably right. I wonder how long it will be."

"Remember when your aunt broke her ankle? She was out of work for six weeks."

"Oh, right. Yes, I remember. That's a long time." She recalled how enthusiastic Teague was about his job and how he had shared most of the details about it on their dinner date. He had reminded her of a little boy at Christmas at the time. "Teague will be miserable sitting at home doing nothing. He loves his job."

"I feel badly for him," Mother commented with no emotion in her voice. "You need to worry about yourself. Sure, you're not skiing now, and some of this couldn't be helped. But you still can't expect to sit there forever with this new friend of yours and think they'll give you all the time off you want."

"I know."

"And watch that he doesn't take advantage of you. Some men would, you know."

"Maybe some men would, but not Teague." Kassia tried to keep the impatience out of her voice. Why did Mother insist on talking to her as though she were unable to use good judgment about any situation in her life? She never treated Deidre and Mona that way. Resentment bubbled near the surface.

"You don't know him that well," Mother pointed out.

"Don't worry, Mother. I'll keep everything under control." She clicked the phone off.

For the first time, she was glad Teague was unconscious. Then he couldn't hear her being given an inquisition by her mother. Irritated, she sat in the chair near Teague's bed and turned on the television to a low volume. Even the national news would be more cheerful than listening to her mother.

Much later Kassia was sitting beside Teague's bed, reading a new magazine she had bought in the hospital gift shop. She heard a knock and looked up to see a woman standing in the doorway. She had Teague's eyes and dark blond hair; only hers boasted a few strands of gray blended into her short but feminine hairstyle. Kassia guessed the woman had to be Teague's mother.

Kassia sent a querying smile. "Hi?"

"Uh, hi. We're looking for Teague Boswell," the woman said tentatively.

Kassia realized the view of Teague's sleeping form was obstructed by a curtain. "He's here." Kassia nodded toward the prone figure in the bed.

The woman entered, followed by a tall man with salt-and-pepper hair, wireless rim glasses, and a mustache. They hurried to the bed. Kassia moved aside to make room for them. Her heart nearly broke when she saw the distress on the woman's face.

"Teague." She reached over and, as Kassia had done earlier, stroked his forehead.

"I'm so sorry," Kassia said.

"Oh. What was I thinking?" The woman turned and smiled at Kassia. "We should have introduced ourselves. I'm Teague's mother, Loretta Boswell. And you must be Kassia Dahl?"

"Yes." She suddenly felt shy. "Nice to meet you."

"You look as lovely as Teague described."

So he had told them about her? "Thank you." Kassia felt her cheeks warm and could only hope she wasn't blushing too readily.

Mrs. Boswell patted the man by her side on the forearm. "This is Teague's father, Dudley."

"Nice to meet you, Mr. Boswell."

"Call me Dudley. Thank you for being here for him." Dudley Boswell's unassuming and gentlemanly manner reminded her of Teague.

"And call me Loretta, of course. Can you tell us what happened?" she asked.

Despite Kassia's reluctance to relive the trauma, she gave his parents her version of the facts.

Loretta touched her arm. "I'm so glad you were there for him." Her eyes misted.

Kassia felt her own eyes threaten to spill tears as she watched their obvious love for him. She could tell they weren't putting on a show for her. Their emotion was genuine. She could feel the spirit of that love envelop the room.

"I think I'll step out for a bite to eat in the cafeteria," Kassia offered.

Loretta took her hand. "Poor thing. You haven't eaten all day, have you?"

"Don't worry about me. I had a muffin for breakfast, and I grabbed a candy bar from the hospital gift shop."

Loretta took in a breath. "That's not enough to keep a bird alive."

"I'm fine. I couldn't have eaten a big meal even if I'd had a chance."

"Too much excitement," Loretta said. "I understand."

"I'll be back soon. Can I get you anything?"

"No, thanks. We don't feel like eating either."

"I understand," she said, repeating his mother's words.

Teague's parents smiled. Their small gesture made her feel a connection to them immediately. No wonder Teague was so compassionate and such an able ambassador for Christ. He had two fine examples to emulate in his parents.

Kassia was on her way to the cafeteria when she nearly bumped into another woman hurrying down the hall. "Pardon me."

"No, excuse me." She touched Kassia's arm. "Could you direct me to room 404?"

Teague's room!

Kassia studied the blond stranger. She felt a wave of jealousy when she saw the woman was not much younger than she was. Even worse, she looked much more beautiful than Kassia thought she could ever hope to be. Whoever she was, Kassia was sure she didn't like her. Not one little bit.

eight

"Um, if you don't know where the room is, that's fine," the young woman said, her voice pleasant. "I'll keep looking."

Kassia wished she would just keep looking right on out the door and as far away from Teague as possible. Yet if she in truth was Teague's friend, Kassia realized she would look petty if she didn't give her directions.

"Wait," she said in a voice commanding enough to stop the woman midstride. "Yes, I know where it is. I was just there. Go to the end of the hall here and make a right. It's two doors down on the left."

The woman brightened. "Good! So I was close after all." She shook her head. "The signs here are so confusing, and with his injuries I wasn't sure where to look. I didn't know if he was in the head-trauma unit or surgery or what. I've already checked two different rooms, and he'd been moved from both. What a wild goose chase."

"You certainly are persistent."

"Apparently persistence pays off, I'm happy to say." Her musical laugh irritated Kassia. "I drove three hours to get here. I wasn't about to give up now."

"Oh." Who would drive three hours to see Teague without a strong connection to him?

"Silly me. I've been babbling. I'm Tabitha Boswell," the woman explained as though she had just reached into Kassia's mind and read it like a book. "I'm looking for my brother, Teague."

"Oh." Kassia paused as the information sank into her brain. "Oh!" She knew relief probably showed itself in her expression.

89

This time she felt her entire face grow warm, a sure sign she had turned a brilliant shade of red.

She studied Tabitha's face and realized the resemblance. Teague had mentioned his sister. Tabitha was successful, the pride of their family. Why hadn't Kassia realized who she was right away?

"I'm so glad I ran into someone who could help me." She smiled brightly. "I couldn't even find the nurses' station on this floor. I thought I'd be wandering the halls all day looking for him."

"Well, you're almost there now. Your parents are with him."

"Good. But they'll probably wonder why I'm so late. I had to close the store before I could leave." She studied Kassia. "You said you were just there? Hey, you must be Kassia."

Kassia's mouth dropped open. So Teague had thought she was important enough to mention to his sister? "Uh, yes. Yes, I am." She decided that giving Tabitha her most charming smile might not hurt.

"It's nice to meet you." Tabitha extended her hand. Her cologne, which smelled of jasmine and vanilla, wafted toward Kassia.

She reached out and shook Tabitha's hand. "It's nice to meet you, too."

Tabitha's gaze bored into Kassia but not in an unfriendly way. She released Kassia's hand. "You know what? You are just as pretty as he said you were."

"Pretty?" Kassia placed her hand to the hollow of her throat. "Really? He said that?"

"Yes, really. I hope you don't mind my telling you. But don't let him know I said it. He'd kill me. I'm sure he's trying to make you think he's calm, cool, and indifferent." Tabitha giggled.

"He's cool, but in a good way," Kassia said. "He's a gentleman, and I appreciate that. Believe me. But he really did say that?"

"I don't know why Teague didn't have the courage to tell you himself that you look like a model." She rolled her eyes and shook her head. "My brother."

Kassia's eyes widened. "A model?"

"Yes, he said you look like a model. And I agree."

"I guess all I can say is thanks!"

Kassia marveled at how such a dazzling woman—who looked like a model herself—could express such an opinion.

Tabitha stood tall, carrying herself with a confident air that somehow conveyed no arrogance. She was dressed in an imaginative outfit, no doubt from her boutique: a ruffled blouse and skirt, with matching suede boots and a leather purse decorated with flowers. Her smooth hair was styled away from her refined face. Kassia felt underdressed in her ski clothes. If Tabitha weren't so friendly and warm—and Teague's sister rather than a rival—Kassia would have felt intimidated.

I'll bet Tabitha and Teague never squabble or show petty jealousies. Not the way my sisters and I do.

"I'm on my way to the cafeteria right now," she said. "I'm sure your parents will be glad you're here."

"Thanks, Kassia. I'll look forward to seeing more of you." Tabitha turned and headed down the hall.

Kassia felt pensive as she boarded the elevator. Why couldn't she have a nice sister like Tabitha? Why couldn't her family be like the Boswells? Kassia speculated that they were the type of Christian family who really loved God, not like hers. Her family was never close, even though they claimed to love God. A verse she had memorized long ago, in Romans, came to mind: *"Accept one another, then, just as Christ accepted you, in order to bring praise to God."*

As far as she could remember, her family never acted as though they accepted one another. At least Mother never accepted that Kassia could think for herself or make intelligent decisions. Yet she was free with praise for her favorite child, Deidre. Father was partial to Mona. When Kassia was clearly in the right, he offered her a halfhearted ally at best. Neither Mona nor Deidre seemed to want Kassia's respect or friendship, since both of them were so busy trying to stay in their parents' good graces by proving themselves to be superspiritual. Unable to compete in the contest for Best Dahl Family Saint, once she entered college, Kassia gave up on church and ever finding fulfillment or solace in spirituality.

If only her family could have accepted Kassia as she was, free-spirited and fun-loving as a child and later as a teen, a person who asked questions—sometimes hard questions. Perhaps then they could have learned more about God together. Instead she received only stern looks and admonitions for her questions.

She had never meant to be disrespectful. She felt a love for God deep in her heart, whether in or out of church. She couldn't understand why her parents acted as though they had to work night and day to gain His approval. They seemed to put church work before everything else, including her. So when Kassia rebelled against her parents, they believed she was at war with God, as well. Her sisters got in on the act and chastised Kassia, too. Before long, Kassia believed her family, along with the principalities of heaven, stood against her in a war she could never win.

Had she been at war with God? Was she still fighting battles with Him, battles she could not win? Or had she let her family's anger with her interfere with her relationship with her creator?

ã

When Teague regained consciousness, he felt only relentless throbbing in his head. What day was it? Oh yes. Monday. He had to get to work!

No, it couldn't be Monday. He was still at the ski resort.

The kids must be wondering why he overslept.

No, wait. He hadn't overslept. The last thing he remembered was waving to Kassia before he pushed off to ski one last time before they had to leave.

Kassia. Just the thought of her helped ease the pain in his head.

He opened his eyes and saw a white ceiling that must have been ten times brighter than the one at the ski resort. What was that beeping sound? He turned his head. A heart monitor? What was going on here?

"Kassia?"

"Teague!" He heard footsteps approaching his bed. "You're awake! Oh, I'm so happy!"

"Of course I'm awake. Why do you seem so surprised?"

"You don't remember?" Kassia asked.

"The last thing I remember was being on the ski slope. Everything after that is a blur."

"That's okay. You'll probably remember more later." He could see her swallow. Her eyes glistened with moisture. She reached down and stroked his arm. "Now don't worry about anything. I'm just glad you're awake."

The light shining in her eyes was unmistakable, and it wasn't from the tears in her eyes. He'd seen that kind of glow before—in his old girlfriend's eyes, long before she left him for some jock she met in school.

But that was then. This was now. Now he was seeing a beautiful woman looking him in the eyes. A woman who obviously cared about him or she wouldn't be here in the hospital with him. Maybe it was love. But he wasn't sure he wanted Kassia falling in love with him. On the trip her faith seemed to be growing, but he thought her relationship with the Lord might still be shaky. His head hurt too much to think about it all now, though.

"Kassia." His voice came out as a whisper.

He heard more footsteps as someone entered the room.

"Loretta!" Kassia said. "He's awake!"

His mother rushed to his side and leaned over his bed. "Teague! Oh, I'm so relieved!" Tears flowed down her cheeks.

"Mom? What are you doing here?" A surge of fear shot through him. If Mom had come all this way, his condition must be serious. "Where's Dad?"

"He stepped out for a snack. He'll be back soon," Mom said.

"What happened to me?"

Kassia turned to him. "I was right behind you and watched. You had just pushed off and started down the hill when it looked to me like your ski hit something under the snow in the path."

Teague lifted his hand to his head. "Oh yeah. . .I remember that."

"Then you must remember how you lost your balance then veered off the path and ran into some trees."

Out of control. . .couldn't stop. . .trees. . .snow. . .blackness.

His heart started pounding in his ears, and he grimaced. "No wonder I ended up here."

"I'm just glad you weren't going any faster. I think that kept you from doing even more damage to your head," Kassia said.

"Praise the Lord for that. How are you feeling now?" Teague's mother asked.

He looked at her. "My head hurts. And, now that you ask, I notice my foot doesn't feel so hot."

Loretta and Kassia exchanged looks then glanced at Teague.

"You broke your ankle," Loretta said.

"Yowzah! No wonder it hurts."

"I'm sure now that you're awake they can give you something for that."

"We need to let someone know. I'll get a nurse," Kassia offered.

His mom watched Kassia leave the room then turned to him. "You know something? That girl has been here the whole time. She was here when we arrived. She never left your side except for a few minutes."

Teague didn't know what to say. He knew they had strengthened their connection during the ski trip, but apparently he hadn't realized how much. Maybe Kassia was turning out to be a true friend after all.

≈

Teague tried to think of something, anything, to put his tension at bay. Nothing seemed to work. He closed his eyes and recited the Lord's Prayer over and over in his mind.

The scent of gardenia perfume drifted toward him. His visitor, whose footfalls he hadn't heard, could only be Kassia. He opened his eyes.

"It's time," Kassia said.

She appeared as a vision in a red sweater.

"Hey. How was the hotel? Comfortable, I hope," he said.

"Just wonderful. But don't you worry about me." She reached over and patted his arm then pulled back her hand. "Are you ready for surgery?"

"As ready as I'll ever be." He reached for her hand. She responded with a warm clasp, her fingers delicate but firm around his. The prospect of surgery was not a welcome one, but he felt better with her by his side. "Kassia, you've been too good to me."

Too good. More than he deserved. He had to tell her not to wait on him or for him. "Kassia, I—"

"What is it?" She squeezed his hand. The comfort of her touch was so appealing.

The words wanted to form on his lips, but they couldn't. "I–I want to thank you—for being here."

≈

In what seemed to be the blink of an eye, Teague awoke from

surgery. He lay on a bed in a tiny space surrounded by a mauve-colored curtain. From somewhere nearby, perhaps on the other side of the curtain, he could hear a man praying in a minister's cadence over a patient. The idea comforted Teague; he knew people were praying for him, too.

A nurse appeared, offered him some water from a cup with a bent straw, and asked if he wanted to see his mother. "Sure," he said faintly. He wondered about Kassia but didn't ask.

Moments later his mother stood inside the curtain. "How are you feeling, honey?"

Teague tried to smile. "Not so hot."

"I can imagine." She stepped to his side and spoke in a hushed voice. "The doctor said everything went well and you should be fine. I'm so relieved. We've all been so worried. Kassia especially. She's been here the whole time. You know, you're lucky to have someone like her as a girlfriend."

Girlfriend? He hadn't thought of her as a girlfriend. Yet when his mother expressed the idea aloud, he liked the sound of it.

"She's quite charming," Mom said. "And you know what? I think she has a good soul."

A good soul. Yes, he supposed she did. Yet he wondered if that soul was truly trusting the Lord. "Are you sure you aren't being nice since I've just come out of surgery?"

"No, I'm not." His mother smiled.

So Kassia had Mom's approval. But Mom didn't know Kassia and how she had lapsed in her faith walk. Would she be so approving if she did?

nine

Kassia picked up the phone on her desk at work.

"Hey, Kassia, do you have a minute?" a peppy voice asked.

"Lexie! For you, yes." Kassia lowered her voice so her nearby coworkers wouldn't know she was on a personal call. "It's been busy this morning, so I might have to put you on hold more while we talk."

"No problem. I know you're at work. And so am I, for that matter." Lexie chuckled. "I've only got a few minutes before I have to be in a meeting. I just thought I'd take an unscheduled break and call you long enough to find out how everything went on the ski trip with Teague. I tried to reach you at home yesterday, but you never picked up the phone or answered your e-mail."

"Oh, I'm so bad about checking my e-mail. You know that, right?" She chuckled.

"I do recall," Lexie agreed.

"And as for the phone, I haven't been home to answer it. Why didn't you leave a message?"

"You know how terrible I am at leaving messages," Lexie said. "I hate talking to a machine. I feel like such an idiot."

"I do recall," Kassia answered in a deliberate but kind imitation of Lexie. The two friends laughed.

"So," Lexie asked, "did you extend your trip?"

"Sort of, but not because we wanted to. We had a lot of fun until the last ten minutes." Kassia told her about Teague's accident.

"Oh, that's awful," Lexie sympathized. "Too bad a great time had to be spoiled at the last minute. How is Teague?"

"As well as can be expected, I guess. He's at home, but I haven't been to visit him yet. Loretta's still there."

"Loretta?"

"His mom."

"Sounds like you two are getting along pretty well if you're already on a first-name basis."

"I don't know. She seems like a friendly person who'd let anyone call her by her first name. But I do like her." Kassia picked up a pencil from the holder and twirled it around in her fingers. "Sometimes I think I get along with her better than I do my own mom." Kassia grimaced. "In fact I know I do. And I met his sister, Tabitha. She's super nice. One in a million." Kassia sighed. She knew Lexie would understand her meaning. They were close, and Lexie was aware that Kassia and her family didn't see eye-to-eye.

"Don't wish for something that can never be," Lexie cautioned. "Everyone else's family might seem to be perfect on the outside, but no one's is."

"You're right. But it's nice to think someone in this world has a great life, isn't it?"

"You can have a great life, too, and maybe Teague can help with that," Lexie said.

"Teague is a good man, a special man. But he's just a friend."

"Since you were so good about staying with him at the hospital, maybe he saw how wonderful you are," Lexie said. "And you're right. Teague is a good man. But don't sell yourself short. You're a good woman. I'm sure he can see that. Maybe he'd like to be more than just friends."

"I don't know," Kassia said. "I can't imagine myself with the type of Christian who can feel a sense of peace just from talking with God."

"Why not? I'm that type of Christian."

"Maybe, but that's different," Kassia said. "Lexie, you've been through a lot with me. I know you weren't too crazy about Brad. And I have to admit, you were right. I'm so glad I didn't let things go too far with him."

"You didn't?"

"Of course not," she said sharply. "Why would you think otherwise?"

"I don't know. I guess because you didn't want me around when he planned to come over."

Kassia knew Lexie was leaving much unsaid. Her faith wasn't as strong as it had once been. Perhaps she deserved for her friends to think the worst of her. She decided to change the subject somewhat. "He's wanted to see me again, and I've turned him down."

"Really? Good for you. I guess it's really none of my business, but, well, I can't help but wonder, Kassia—how far did you let things go with Brad?"

"What is that supposed to mean?" Kassia snapped. "Look— I might not be as close to God as you are, but that doesn't mean I let guys get away with much."

"I guess I was thinking about that verse in the Bible that says to 'avoid every kind of of evil.' "

"Are you serious? Do I appear evil?" Kassia was surprised and hurt that her best friend would imply such a thing.

"Well, do you remember that night you and Brad were kissing in the restaurant when the four of us double-dated?" Lexie asked.

Kassia shuddered. "Maybe that didn't look so good. You know, I'm sorry I kissed him at all, much less in public. And I'm sorry if I embarrassed you and Theo."

"Don't worry about it. I understand."

Kassia realized then that Lexie's forgiveness and friendship were more important to her than Brad's attention ever was.

"Just think about the men you choose in the future."

"But you can't help who you love."

"Are you so sure? At some point in a relationship, you

choose whether or not to pursue it. Somewhere between first attraction and seeing each other's flaws," Lexie said.

Kassia thought for a moment. "I see what you mean."

"You have to think about why you pursue the wrong men."

"Now wait just a minute. I'm old enough to decide who's right for me and who's wrong."

"I know. But I only want you to think more carefully next time before jumping in. Will you do that? For me?"

Kassia shook her head. "Only you can get away with telling me that, because I know you care about me." Her voice softened. "Thanks."

Kassia was grateful for Lexie's concern, but her frank advice unsettled her. What if Lexie was right? She started to consider the possibilities.

"Hey." Lexie's voice interrupted her thoughts. "It's not as if you haven't been there for me."

Kassia knew Lexie would always be thankful for her help after her first husband died. Lexie and her daughter had shared Kassia's second bedroom when they moved back to town and needed to start a new life. "I was glad to help," Kassia said. "And I'll always be there for you."

Kassia didn't wait for Lexie to answer. Instead she brightened her voice and changed the subject to two topics she was sure her friend never tired of. "So how is Theo? And does Piper still like school?"

Lexie took the hint and talked about how well her life was progressing. Soon Kassia had caught up on the news then reluctantly ended the conversation. She placed the receiver in its cradle. At least someone had a perfect life. But why couldn't she have one, too?

❧

A week later Teague lounged on his couch, watching daytime television. He didn't want to get involved in any soap opera plots and clicked past those stations. The talk shows only interested him slightly. He could choose between trying to catch up in the middle of an old movie, watching a thirty-year-old adventure series, or getting bored with a game show repeat. If someone had told him two weeks before that he'd be hanging around his house on a Monday, watching reruns of old game shows, he never would have believed it.

His mother entered the living room from where she had been washing lunch dishes. She had agreed to help Teague for a week, but this was her last day before she had to return to teaching kindergarten. Dad would pick her up this evening and take her home. Teague didn't know exactly how he would survive after she left, but he would figure out something. He had gotten himself into the situation, even though unintentionally, so would cope with the consequences.

His mother sat down in the brown leather chair near the couch. "Honey, are you just going to lie there while you're at home and watch game shows?"

"I don't know. I might change the channel if they start showing repeats of repeats." He grinned.

Teague was determined to keep his sense of humor. His situation wouldn't have been happy in the best of circumstances, but without a job, being laid up was even worse. If he had still been employed, someone would have sent materials home to him so he could work on his laptop. But now, with no income and nothing to do, being at home wasn't as relaxing or enjoyable as he had envisioned.

The prospect of having little money was even more worrisome. The health insurance he had with his old job was scheduled to run out in a month. But even with the majority of his hospital expenses covered, he still needed to meet his other obligations. He desperately wanted to rejoin the ranks of the employed, but the most he'd been able to accomplish in his search for a new job while he recuperated was to use the phone and Internet. Personal interviews seemed impossible.

Besides, who would want to hire an injured man?

"How about a book?" his mother asked, interrupting his musings. "I can go to the library and check out something for you. Science fiction, maybe? That would take your mind off yourself."

"Thanks, but I don't need you to go to all that trouble. I'm okay."

"You're okay?" She raised her eyebrows. "You can't fool me. I'm your mother. I can look at your face and tell when you're worried. Now don't fret so much," she told him. "I know it's hard, but we will do all we can to help you out."

"You've done enough just by being here for me through this injury."

"I've been blessed by this time with you." She leaned over and patted the knee on his unharmed leg. "Besides, you'll be back on your feet and working before you know it."

Teague wasn't sure what to say. Whenever he tried to hide anything from either of his parents, the news always came out. He couldn't help but recall Matthew 10:26, *"There is nothing concealed that will not be disclosed, or hidden that will not be made known."*

"I wish everything would be that easy," he admitted.

"Of course healing from such a major injury won't be easy," Mom said. "You'll be on crutches for a while." She thumped her hand on the arm of the chair. "I know. Why don't I run by your office and pick up some work for you? That would take your mind off everything and let you get something done, too."

"Uh, thanks, but I don't need you to do that."

"I don't mind. Really." She got up from the chair and headed toward the phone. "I can call your boss now and let him know I'll be there within the hour."

"Don't do that." His voice came out more sharply than he had intended.

His mother stopped and turned to face him. She opened her mouth slightly, in the way she always did when she wondered what had possessed him, and regarded him with a gaze that pierced right through him.

"There's something you're not telling me." Her lips narrowed into a taut line. "Is your supervisor giving you a hard time about needing this time off?"

"No. In fact he wants me to take time off." Teague stared at his outstretched legs. "Too much time."

"Forced vacation?" She folded her arms and nodded. "I've heard about that. A lot of companies use that tactic to keep from laying people off." She sighed. "I'm sorry to hear they're having such a rough time. But so are a lot of other companies."

"Yes. They are." Teague still couldn't look her in the eye. He struggled with his news. If only he didn't have to tell her anything. But if he wanted to maintain an honest relationship with his parents, he couldn't hide it from them any longer. He braced himself to reveal his plight. His body tensed. "Mom, it's worse for me than that. I wasn't just forced to take vacation. I was let go."

"Let go!" She rushed to the couch and sat on the cushion near his feet. "But you loved your job, and you were working hard. I don't understand."

"Neither do I, if you want to know the truth. But we lost a contract, and Will didn't feel he could afford to keep me on without more work in sight."

Her shoulders drooped. "Oh, Teague. I'm so sorry. When did this happen?"

"Last week, before I went on the ski trip."

"And you've waited all this time to say something?"

He nodded. "I'm sorry. I didn't want to say anything about it because I didn't want you to worry. And now look what I've done. I never should have been so foolish. I never should have gone on such a risky trip, knowing I didn't have a job and my insurance would be running out soon."

"Don't be so hard on yourself," she said. "You know how to ski. How could you have predicted you'd have an accident? From all reports, the tumble you took clearly wasn't your fault. In fact a couple of the people I work with even suggested you might be able to take the owners of the lodge to court."

"I'm not going to do that. It's not worth the trouble, and besides, there's no way to prove an obstacle was in the path." He remembered something else. "Anyway, everyone signed a disclaimer relieving them from responsibility for any mishaps."

"Everyone knows how to cover their bases these days," his mother said. "Not that I blame them. One big loss in court and they could go bankrupt."

"You're right," he agreed. "Even if I had a case, I'm not sure I'd sue. I think sometimes it's right to go to court, but I don't feel that's the way the Lord wants me to spend my time now."

His mother patted his left knee. "I'm so proud of you for listening to Him. The Lord will see you through, as He always does."

"I know, Mom. I've been praying."

"Good. And I want you to know I'll do anything I can to help you on your job search," she said. "I can take time off from work and drive you to your job interviews."

"I can see me hobbling in for an interview right now." Teague groaned.

"They'll know it's not a permanent injury." She smiled. "Of course, the sympathy factor alone might get you a job."

He laughed. "You always know how to cheer me up. But, no, I won't let you take off from work. Besides, I don't have any interviews lined up yet."

"When you do, you let me know."

"Thanks, but that may be awhile. Jobs are scarce right now."

"I know, but someone with your ambition and talent is bound to find something else soon." She tapped the arm of her chair. "What about Kassia? Maybe she knows someone, or maybe her company has a job opening."

"That's a thought." Teague didn't want to admit to his mom that he hadn't told Kassia. Their time together on the ski trip had been limited, and he hadn't wanted to spoil the few minutes they had together sharing such bad news. Just when he thought he was stable enough to settle down, this had to happen. He didn't want to tell her. He was too much of a coward. He prayed she wouldn't find out before he could gather up enough courage to tell her himself.

"Kassia is such a nice girl," his mother observed. "Do you think you could get serious about her?"

"Oh, Mom!" Despite his objections, the suggestion seemed reasonable.

"I was just asking. Look at how she stayed with you at the hospital until after your surgery. You don't see that kind of devotion every day from people you've been friends with for years, much less someone you hardly know." She paused. "Unless you've known her longer than you've let on to us."

"No. We had only been out to dinner once and then the ski trip."

"She must be smitten then."

Teague didn't answer.

"Your dad said he had a wonderful time talking to her when he took her home."

"I'm sure she enjoyed talking with him, too."

"I'm so glad it looks like you might have found someone," Mom said. "I know you've been waiting a long time."

"I know." Teague's voice was soft. How could he express his nagging doubts about Kassia to his mother when Kassia had shown him nothing but kindness?

He watched his mother pick up the newspaper and begin reading. A pleased smile lingered on her face. She had always been good at assessing people's characters. Was it possible he was being too judgmental?

Even if he wasn't, he harbored no expectations beyond friendship. The alliance had been forged because of a temporary setback. True friendships were based on more than just compassion in the face of adversity or on gratitude. He had to remember that.

His worries went far beyond friendships, though. His whole life had shattered. In a few days he had gone from being a valued employee of a promising, dynamic company, to being laid up, recovering from surgery that left him with pins in his ankle. He also wasn't sure how easy finding a new job would be in this tight economy.

I have nothing to offer Kassia.

Her presence at his bedside had comforted him more than he could have anticipated. She stood with him. He now realized how much he wanted a woman in his life, a helpmate rather than a mother or sister.

He thought about the beautiful brunette. Even though she was taking baby steps in her faith walk, any man would be lucky to have her. Brad's obvious interest in her at the restaurant demonstrated that Kassia had her pick of men. She held down a responsible job as an office manager for a group of stockbrokers. Suddenly he felt unworthy again. Why would she want an unemployed, injured man to pull her down?

She shouldn't have to. Without a word, he made a resolution. The next time Kassia called, he would thank her for her help and then make no promises or offers to see her again. The sooner she got on with her own life, the better.

He tightened his lips, but his determined feeling evaporated as soon as it arrived. If he would be better off without Kassia, then why did he feel so heartbroken?

❧

From his perch on the couch, Teague set the Saturday edition of the *Richmond Times Dispatch* aside and looked out the front picture window at the yard. The grass lay dormant, sleeping during the winter months. Three Japanese maple trees, so beautiful with red leaves during the spring and summer months, were stripped of their former glory but stood stalwart in wait for warmer weather. He felt thankful that at least he didn't have to stress over yard work while he recovered.

At intervals, cars, vans, and SUVs whizzed by on the two-lane country road in front of the house. Teague cringed when he noticed several were traveling too fast for the curves. Still, their speed made him long for the freedom of motion once again. At first the rest had been somewhat welcome. The time spent with Mom had given him a chance to reconnect with her in a way he hadn't experienced since he was in high school. But now she had left, and everyone else had gone on with their lives out of necessity. Restlessness visited more often than friends and family.

The white wooden farmhouse across the way was well off the road. In the summer, corn grew in the field in front of the home. Teague hadn't seen hide nor hair of Mr. Wilkins, the farmer who shared some of his vegetable harvest with Teague during the warm summer months. He knew the farmer wasn't aware he had been injured, and he wasn't about to call and worry him. Still, Teague wished Mr. Wilkins would stop in for a chat.

As he mused about his loneliness, he noticed a small blue car slowing down in front of his house. Coming almost to a stop, the car hesitated as though the driver was confirming the number on his mailbox. Just then the car pulled into his driveway. The heavy layer of gravel crackled as the car made its way to the house.

"Who could that be?" he muttered.

Teague didn't like the idea of living so close to other people as many did in the city. He had chosen to rent a home in a rural area that offered a longer but not intolerable commute.

The low density of homes and his long driveway discouraged visitors. He recalled no recent visits from traveling salesmen, missionaries, or children selling goods for fund-raising.

The car didn't belong to his pastor or anyone from church. He didn't recognize it as belonging to a friend, neighbor, or relative. Whether he liked it or not, someone he didn't know had stopped by. He wasn't sure he wanted to take the trouble to hobble to the door.

He clicked his tongue. "I'll bet I know who this is. It must be one of the women from church bringing me something for lunch."

Teague looked down at his clothes and decided he looked presentable enough in a white sweatshirt and black sweat-pants. Knowing he would need time to answer the door, he rose from his seat and tottered to respond to the knock that had not yet come.

He stopped in the middle of his hobbling. "But Mrs. Grue-man from church isn't supposed to be here until tonight."

Curious, he glanced outside and spotted a brunette emerging from the car. Curls escaped from her hooded coat of leopard spots.

He took in a breath. "Kassia!"

His stomach did a flip-flop on seeing her. How could he be so firm in his resolve not to see her anymore when he was alone, but the moment he noticed her in front of his house, he became soft as mush?

Father, where is my strength?

ten

Kassia stared at the small but sturdy brick house. She remembered Teague had mentioned he was renting his home. Noting the expansive lawn, she wondered why anyone would agree to take care of so much land when he didn't even own it. Still, large trees in the yard lent the house a sense of stability and permanence that no apartment complex could offer, no matter how upscale or well planned.

In spite of the cold weather, she took in a deliberate breath. Fresh air!

Leaning on her car door, she paused for a moment in the stillness. Out here in the country she could now understand why a person might like to live away from the hurry of the city. In her apartment she could hear muffled sounds of other tenants talking through the walls she shared with them. Often she would notice her upstairs neighbors walking back and forth across their floor and even hear water running through the pipes behind the wall.

Living out in the country all by himself, Teague had no such problems. Then again Kassia wondered if he ever got lonely.

Realizing she had paused too long, she opened the back door of her small car and retrieved the cardboard box from the floor. She took a minute to inspect her dishes. She was thankful none of the containers had come open and spilled their contents.

Maybe I should have made sure Teague wanted all this food. Maybe I should have been sure he wanted to see me before I barged in.

Whether he wanted to see her or not, she had to try. Ever since she'd left him after surgery, she couldn't get him off her mind. Every day she wanted to call him but resisted the urge. The fact that his mother was staying with him was a welcome deterrent. Kassia had too much pride to look as if she was chasing Teague, even though she and Loretta had taken an instant liking to each other.

Funny how I can get along with his mom. Why can't it be like that with my own mother?

Kassia wondered, though, why she was standing in the freezing cold with a meal she had spent a lot of time and effort on, taking it to a man who hadn't called her once since he'd left the hospital. Yet she felt a sense of peace about what she was doing.

Lord, are You trying to tell me something?

⋧

Teague leaned on his crutches and watched Kassia draw in a breath of air then stop. She studied the side yard, obviously unaware he could see her. He wondered what she was thinking. He smiled. Something about being in the country seemed to make people pause and reflect. And that was a positive thing.

He observed her unload a large cardboard box from her car and was at once reminded of his current helplessness. Ordinarily he would have hurried to her aid. Since he couldn't move with enough agility to meet her at the car, he had to witness her shut the car door with her hip then carefully walk to the front porch with whatever she carried in the box.

He moved as fast as he could to answer the door. At least he could keep her from trying to balance her load and knock at the same time.

"Hi!" he said, opening the door.

"Hi! How's it going?" Kassia's smile was bright.

Better now that you're here.

"I'm so-so," he replied. "I think I'm improving each day, but

I sure wish I could get this cast off."

"You have some time ahead of you," she remarked.

"Yes, I sure do. But visitors make the time go faster." He smiled. "I wasn't expecting you."

"I tried to call before I left the apartment," she said, "but your line was busy."

"Oh yeah. I was checking my e-mail on my laptop."

"Any news?"

He hesitated. He still hadn't mentioned his job loss. How pathetic could he get, looking for responses to his resume on a Saturday morning?

"No news, unless I want to invest in transferring twenty-eight million dollars from a Nigerian bank or lose ten pounds by Valentine's Day."

She chuckled. "Sounds like we're on the same mailing lists."

Kassia's breath made contact with the cold, and steam emitted from her mouth in spurts as she spoke. Suddenly Teague realized he'd forgotten his manners.

"Come in." He pulled to one side so she could enter.

She stepped over the threshold, and when she passed, he could smell the familiar gardenia scent he had grown to love. The floral fragrance mingled with appetizing aromas of food. His stomach grumbled, reminding him that several hours had passed since he'd eaten a bowl of sugary cereal for breakfast.

"Sorry I can't help you with that," he said, pointing to the box. "I'm lucky to be answering the door as it is."

"That's quite all right. I remember how you helped me with my bags while we were on the ski trip." She grinned. "Your credentials as a gentleman remain intact."

He managed a short bow as he leaned on his crutches. "Thank you, milady."

"Do you mind if I take this in to the table?" She nodded toward the dining room, which could be seen from the front door.

"No, that's fine."

He followed her, glancing at the couch where he had spent most of his time lately. He had invested in brown leather, a decision he'd never regretted. The couch was hardly at its best, scattered as it was with two multicolored afghans his grandmother had crocheted years ago, along with a cheap blue woven acrylic blanket he had picked up at a recent sale. Newspapers and magazines were piled not so neatly on the oak end table in front of a white-shaded lamp with a wooden base that matched the table reasonably well. Suddenly he realized every flat surface except the hardwood floor was covered with reading material. Even the coffee table, positioned on the far side of the room so he wouldn't have to go around it when he tried to move about, was burdened with a hodgepodge of papers; a box of tissues; and—he noticed to his horror—his cereal bowl, coffee cup, and juice glass from breakfast. He stifled a groan. At least his mother had dusted and cleaned before she left. If not for her, his embarrassment would have been complete.

They walked through the small dining room with its pine table and chairs. He was glad he'd filled the rooms with furniture, however modest.

He looked at the old flower-patterned wallpaper in the room as though seeing it for the first time. "Um, this isn't my house. The landlord wouldn't be happy with me if I made too many changes," he offered as an apology.

"Changes?" She followed his gaze. "Oh, you mean the wallpaper?" She shrugged. "Looks good to me. At least it's not beige, like the walls in my apartment. I've thought of going wild and painting every wall in the place red, but then I'd have to repaint when I left. I'm too lazy to do that." She winked.

"I don't blame you. I wouldn't want to try to cover red with beige paint." He grimaced. "But you wouldn't really use red paint, would you?"

"Not in every room." She giggled.

He shook his head. He could imagine Kassia, who seemed to wear at least one red item of clothing with every outfit, painting every room in her house a bold shade of crimson.

She reached inside the box and took out a covered brown glass dish. When she lifted its top, the smell of gravy and onions permeated the dining room. "I hope you like beef."

He inhaled a fresh whiff of the gravy. "Love it."

"Good." She took out a white ceramic square dish decorated with red and yellow flowers. "And mashed potatoes." A quick lift of the top revealed a smooth mountain of creamy white spuds.

"Sure do." He licked his lips.

"And salad."

He wasn't quite as sure about green vegetables. "Mmm."

She set a large blue ceramic bowl covered with transparent wrap on the table. "I put in lots of goodies. Carrots, alfalfa sprouts, tomatoes, and mushrooms."

Even more vegetables. Well, except for the mushrooms. "Mmm."

"And I brought salad dressing in case you didn't have any." She held up a bottle of white dressing. "Blue cheese."

Ah. A white stream of hope in the midst of all that green. "My favorite."

"I know. I saw you slathering it on your salad at the lodge."

"So you're observant."

"I try." Her grin was teasing and captivating at once. "I made sure to get low-fat dressing, though."

Too bad.

"Low-fat. Mmm."

"I had to do something to counteract the effects of all that blue cheese since I made dessert." She reached into the box again and withdrew a pie covered in bright red cherries. "Cherry cream cheese."

"Now that sounds—and looks—good." He set his crutches

against the wall then took his customary chair at the head of the table. "But I hope you know you didn't have to do this. My church has been bringing food over here every day. In fact, Emily's mom is supposed to stop by with food tonight."

The light in her eyes vanished, and she hesitated. "Oh. I–I didn't think of that. You must have more food in the house than you can ever eat."

"No, not at all," he said quickly, though he knew his refrigerator was far from empty. "For one thing, no one ever brings lunch. Only dinner. And no one is half as beautiful or charming as you."

He blurted the compliment as a reflexive response since he knew he had hurt her feelings. Yet as he studied her face he realized he had brought the truth to light with his words.

"Oh, I don't believe it," she said, her eyes bright again and her face flushed.

"You know who the most beautiful person in my church is?" He didn't wait for her to speculate on who it could be. "It's Miss Patricia."

"Miss Patricia? Who is that?"

"She's a dear eighty-five-year-old woman. Her married name is Henderson, but she tells us to call her Miss Patricia because Mrs. Henderson was her mother-in-law."

Kassia's laugh added music to the room. "She sounds like a pistol."

"She sure is. Her specialty is baking cakes. She takes a big cake to anyone in church who is sick or grieving or in some sort of need."

"Now, I have to say, she does sound like a lovely woman," Kassia agreed.

"You know what's unbelievable? She embellishes each cake with a Bible verse, and it looks like a professional decorated it."

"And she's eighty-five?"

"Eighty-five."

"And she writes a whole verse on a cake? Wow."

"Granted, it's always a short verse," he pointed out, "but a verse all the same."

" 'Jesus wept'?" Kassia smiled.

"I haven't seen one with that verse so far." Just then he snapped his fingers several times rapidly. "Quick. Quick. Tell me why He wept."

She thought for a moment. "Because His friend Lazarus died."

Teague whistled. "Whoa. That's right."

She placed her hands on her hips. "You didn't think I'd know that, did you? I still remember a few things from all the Sunday school classes I attended over the years."

"You remind me of Lazarus," Teague said. "Not that you've died, of course"—he grinned—"but because you're such a good friend. Won't you eat this wonderful food with me?"

Her mouth dropped open. "I—uh—"

"Unless you have other plans."

"Well, no."

"You drove all the way from Richmond. You deserve to eat," he pointed out. "Besides, if you don't stay, I'll have to eat alone. You wouldn't wish that on me, would you?" He widened his eyes and pouted.

"Oh, please. That puppy dog act may work on your other girlfriends, but not on me." She shook her head.

"What other girlfriends? Now you're making me even more sad." He sniffled. "Especially since this is enough food for ten people."

"Well, I admit, I wasn't sure if you'd be having family visiting since it's Saturday. I thought maybe Tabitha would be dropping by."

"Not on a Saturday. That's her busiest day at the boutique."

Kassia tapped herself on the forehead. "Of course. What was I thinking?" She inspected the table laden with food. "Oh, all right. I'll take pity on you and stay." She flashed him a big smile then slipped off her coat. "Where can I hang this up?"

"There's a coat closet right by the front door. I should help you—"

She waved her hand. "Oh, no. I can find it. You sit down and get ready for some comfort food."

"If you insist." He grinned. The fact of the matter was, he thoroughly enjoyed being waited on. The meals from church were a tremendous help, but he had to set the table and clean up. Without someone to share the work, doing the chores was a lonely prospect.

The dinner was one of the best he'd eaten since he'd broken his ankle, both in the quality of the food and the company. The more time he spent with Kassia, the less resolve he felt to let her slip out of his life. But she'd been hurt enough. Why should he add to her pain?

But he felt he had to broach the subject, if only in a roundabout way. After dessert he leaned back in his chair and patted his stomach. "That was great. I won't have any room for dinner after such a big lunch, but who cares?"

"That's what your refrigerator is for," she said, chuckling.

He placed his elbows on the table and looked her in the eyes. "I may tease you about bringing over all this food, but you know what? You aren't obligated to do anything for me. There was nothing you could have done to prevent my accident."

She shuddered. "I'll never forget what I saw."

He resisted the urge to place his hand on hers. "I'm sorry. I wish you hadn't had to see it."

"No, I'm glad I did. At least I was there to draw attention to the fact that you were hurt."

"True. I can't help but wonder, though, if I'd have lain there all day had it not been for you."

"You think people would have skied by and not stopped?

Anyway, the ski patrol guys were right there, almost as soon as you fell."

"Yeah, and I'm sure glad they were. But most people would have been concentrating on getting down the slope and not looking at the forest."

"True."

"But my point is that I hope you don't feel responsible for me. I've had my share of attention." He grinned. "As you can tell, even my family members have gone back to their lives."

"I know, but I want to be here. Unless I'm a bother."

"Are you kidding? I appreciate it. Bringing me food, making sure I'm still alive, giving me someone to talk to. I'm the one who doesn't want to be a bother to you."

"It's no bother. I only live a few miles away, remember?" She grinned. "And speaking of miles, I was wondering when you were going to ask me for a ride to work. It's been a week since you left the hospital. Your boss may be wonderful, but I doubt he'll let you lie around here indefinitely without doing any work."

Teague hesitated. Since he had revealed the news to his mother, telling it again seemed a little easier. "I guess I'd better tell you. I was hoping I'd find something else before you had to find out."

"Find out what?"

"I was laid off." There. He said it.

"You're kidding! But I thought your boss liked you."

"He does. But we lost the contract I was working on, and his operation is too lean for him to keep me on."

Her gaze softened, and her voice held an anxious tone. "When did this happen?"

"Just before we went on the ski trip. I didn't want to say anything then. Besides, we barely knew each other."

"What a difference a couple of weeks make, huh?"

Teague smiled. The only good thing about the accident was

that it had shown him a part of Kassia's character he otherwise might not have seen—her sisterly love and compassion.

"That's awful about your job, and especially now. I'm so sorry. I know you really liked working for them. Have you told your family?"

He nodded. "I told Mom. She understands. My family knows I'm a hard worker and being laid off isn't my fault."

"Lucky you. If I had been in your shoes, my parents would have lectured me and convinced me I'd done something terribly wrong."

Teague leaned over and tapped his cast. "I do have the sympathy factor."

"That wouldn't have stopped my mom from lecturing me." She shook her head. "You really are lucky. Your family acts a lot more Christian than mine, even though my parents are the first ones at church every time the doors open."

"My family does set a good example, but try not to be so hard on yours," Teague said. "I'm sure they're doing the best they can."

She stared across the room. Teague saw her gaze settle on a cheap print of an original oil painting of fruit. For the first time, he wished he hadn't economized on wall decorations. But then he realized she was looking through the picture as if it didn't exist.

"I'm sure they are, in their own way." Her words seemed directed not to him but to someone he couldn't see. Suddenly she turned to him. "I don't want to talk about them. I'm more interested now in what I can do to help you find a new job."

"Not much. I've got resumes out."

"Good." She smiled. "I know it's nerve-racking, but you're not the only one. People lose their jobs all the time nowadays. Once upon a time, you could leave the only place you ever worked at with a gold watch after fifty years. But no more." She paused and smiled again. "But at least that allows everyone to keep fresh and interested in our work."

"That's you, Kassia. Always looking on the bright side, even when there isn't one."

"Sure there is. You're talented and in a good profession. You'll find something soon. And I'll do everything I can to help you."

❧

Kassia kept true to her word. She seemed more determined than ever to do what she could. She hovered over Teague, helping him every step of the way. Each day she stopped by his house before work, prepared breakfast, and made sure he had food ready to heat for lunch. Even though the church had been great about providing Teague with food, he still needed some extra items such as soda and juice, and she kept his refrigerator stocked without even asking him. She came over most evenings and helped him set up whatever meal had been provided, tidied up, and did his laundry.

Sometimes she brought a DVD for them to watch. Not so long ago, he would have been leery about trusting her to select a movie without questionable elements. But he soon discovered they enjoyed the same types of films. To keep their movie nights interesting, Kassia chose Westerns on Tuesdays and mysteries on Saturdays.

Teague's youth group met on Sunday afternoons, and now that he was laid up, the meetings had moved to his house.

"Why don't you join us tomorrow afternoon?" he asked Kassia. It was two Saturdays later, after a delicious lunch she had brought—hot potato soup and a croissant sandwich stacked high with thinly sliced beef. He felt fortified enough to ask her to be more involved in his life.

She wagged her finger at him. "Oh no you don't. You're not going to recruit me to be your coleader. You can handle them much better than I ever could. Not to mention, my Bible knowledge hardly compares with yours."

He laughed. "I wasn't trying to recruit you. But since you mentioned it, wouldn't you like to be our mascot?"

"No, wearing silly outfits isn't my idea of fun." She wrinkled her nose. "I'll see you Tuesday."

"Hey, you didn't say anything about being busy tomorrow night."

"Tomorrow night, huh?" She touched her finger to her chin and tapped it several times. "Um, I think I can clear my schedule. What do you have in mind?"

"How about a comedy? Or maybe we can take a look at a movie by a director we haven't seen."

"That's a thought. I have to say, I haven't brushed up on this much movie knowledge since film class in college." She grinned. "That was one of my favorite courses."

Teague felt a surge of happiness. Since Kassia's visits had become regular, he wondered what she did on the nights she wasn't with him. He didn't dare ask, though. No need to make her think he was possessive.

"I'll bone up on directors and pick one or two movies to try out," he said.

"Make sure you pick someone from the Golden Age of Hollywood," she told him.

"Will do." Watching her put on the leopard-print coat that had become so familiar, he waved to her from his chair and wished he could help her with it.

Teague was more than happy with his assignment, and he wasn't surprised by her suggestion to stick to vintage films. Never could he have shown an old movie to his youth group; they favored modern fare. He didn't want to suggest recreation that would discourage anyone from attending. But being around Kassia made him realize he had missed spending time with someone his age. She was the first person he'd found who shared his interests, especially his eclectic tastes in entertainment, and he felt blessed.

The woman he had resolved to set free from a worldly existence had turned out to be his rescuer. To his surprise, Teague thanked the Lord for her.

≥●

Kassia was whistling a cheery tune as she walked down the hall to her apartment. Her heels, which usually clicked on sidewalks and hard floors, were silent on the green carpet. Thoughts of the evening with Teague filled her head with pleasant new memories. Now she looked forward to a hot shower and a cup of herbal tea before she retired for the night.

Rounding the corner, she noticed a man holding a bouquet of flowers. She could just make out his face under the dim light above her door.

Brad! What is he doing here?

eleven

Kassia slowed her footsteps almost to a halt.

Why was Brad leaning against the wall outside her apartment? She wished she could escape, but he'd already seen her and waved. Even from that distance she could see his features were terse.

Whatever he had to say, she had a feeling she didn't want to hear it. She felt she had no choice, though, except to keep going. Not too fast and not too slow. She didn't want to seem eager to get the encounter over with or give him the impression she lacked confidence.

It seemed to take forever to get there. But enough time to paste a half smile on her face, not too friendly, not too cool. "Hi, Brad. I wasn't expecting you."

"Obviously. I've been waiting here awhile now. I thought I'd drop by and see how you were doing."

Waiting? Her body tensed. "You weren't waiting too long, I hope."

"Longer than I would have liked."

"Well, you can see I'm doing very well. Now if you'll excuse me." She jingled her keys in her pocket and hoped the sound would encourage him to go.

His eyes narrowed. "Aren't you going to invite me in? I came all this way."

"I'm sorry, but it's late, and I need to get to bed. I have an early day tomorrow."

"Tomorrow is Sunday. Where do you have to go?"

"Church."

"Church? Don't lie to me. I know you don't go to church. If

I remember correctly, you were at odds with your last room-mate because you weren't religious enough for her." He spit out the words.

"I—I've changed my mind. I grew up in the church but had turned away from God when you met me. Not that I'm any great Christian now." She stared at the tips of her toes as though they needed fresh polish. Admitting a fault to Brad stung her, but if she was going to change, she had to make up her mind not to be a hypocrite.

"So you found God?" He folded his arms. "Funny how so many people find God. Seems to me He stays lost an awful lot."

Kassia sensed Brad thought he was being cute, but she refused to give him the satisfaction of even a small grin. She tried to escape again. "As I said, it's time for me to go."

"Where were you?"

"Where was I?" How did Brad dare ask her such a personal question? Suddenly she realized any feelings she may have harbored for him had dissolved. Even his considerable physical attributes no longer appealed to her.

"Have you lost your hearing? Were you at a noisy bar?" he prodded. "I've been to more than my share of those. They can be hard on the ears."

His tone lightened, indicating he was taking a stab at showing sympathy. Yet Kassia's gut told her any compassionate feelings he displayed were far from sincere.

She decided not to fall for his ploy. "Um, I'm sorry, but where I spend my time is none of your business."

He reached over and grabbed her arm. "You were with that guy."

Kassia could feel her heart throbbing, not with the fondness she felt when she was with Teague, but with an icy terror. Mentally she ran through her options if Brad turned violent. From her peripheral vision she noticed the apartment door across the way. Mr. Jones was always home early on Saturday nights. He would hear her scream. And scream she would, if Brad gripped her any tighter.

"I was with a friend. That's all you need to know. In fact that's more than you need to know." She lowered her voice. "Now let me go," she said between her clenched teeth.

He stared into her eyes. Knowing the situation could grow ugly if she let down her resistance, she didn't blink.

Please, Lord, send help!

Brad let go of her arm and stepped back but stayed close enough so she could still smell his cologne. The musky scent, once appealing, turned her stomach.

"Since I've been waiting here for over an hour, the least you can do is let me in." His voice was more conciliatory, coaxing the words into a purr.

"I already told you I need to get to bed." She wished she had chosen another way to say it.

He opened his mouth to speak, no doubt to offer a proposition.

"Alone." Her voice was frigid.

Kassia was so busy warding off Brad that she didn't hear her neighbor approach. She looked over Brad's shoulder and saw the man, another tenant she knew by sight though not by name. Often he would jog around the complex, and judging by his bulky physique the man belonged to a gym somewhere.

He must have seen panic in her eyes and stance because he paused. "Is everything all right here?"

She hesitated. How should she answer?

"Everything's fine. I'm just having a conversation with my friend," Brad said.

The neighbor studied Kassia's face. "Do you agree with that?"

"Uh, I was telling Brad good night." Kassia looked at Brad. "Good night, Brad."

She watched Brad's eyes focus on her, then on her neighbor, and back on her.

"Good night, Brad." Her voice was stronger, with her neighbor there to give her courage.

"Fine." He threw the bouquet of flowers he was holding on the floor. Daisies, baby's breath, and greenery splayed all over the hall carpet.

She stood still and fought the impulse to pick up the poor flowers.

"I'll be back another time."

Kassia decided it might be a good idea to let her neighbor know Brad was no longer a friend. "Don't bother," she said loudly enough for Brad to hear. "If you do, I'll have no choice but to call the police."

She watched him walk away without looking back.

"Hey," her neighbor said gently. "A man doesn't throw a bouquet of flowers on the floor unless he's very upset. Are you going to be okay?"

She nodded. "I think so."

Since Brad was out of sight and unlikely to return, she bent down to pick up the flowers, and the man knelt to help her. "Thank you," she told him.

He handed her several daisies and a broken fern. "No problem."

She took the flowers from him and tried to arrange them in better order. "I'm sorry you had to see that," she said, wrapping the lace-printed cellophane paper around them. "But I'm glad you came along when you did."

He looked down the hallway even though Brad had disappeared. "So am I. You let me know if he bothers you again."

"Thanks, but I don't think he will. He could see we look out for each other here." She had no way of knowing if he was a believer, but she couldn't resist adding, "You know something? Your coming by when you did was an answer to prayer."

"Prayer?" His doubtful grin revealed a missing tooth. "Yeah, right."

"Yeah. Right." She repeated his words firmly.

"Think what you want to, but I'm no angel."

"Think what you want, but I'd like to give you these as a way of saying 'thank you.'" She handed him the daisies.

"Me with flowers?" He threw back his head and let out a laugh that filled the corridor.

Despite his scoffing, Kassia had a feeling he would enjoy the blooms. One thing she knew for certain—almost anyone would benefit from them more than she would. Just seeing the innocent daisies would remind her of the argument with Brad.

"Take them," she implored. "Please? I won't tell anyone."

He shrugged. "Okay. Why not? Maybe even I could use a little reminder of Mother Nature in the apartment." He accepted the flowers. "Thanks."

"You're welcome."

He waved to her and walked away. "See you later."

"Yeah. See you later."

Despite her shaking hands, Kassia turned the key to her apartment and hurried in. She closed the door with a loud *thump*, as if she were shutting the door on her relationship with Brad. If only she didn't have to see him at work. She hoped he would have the decency to avoid her there.

Once she had entered the safety of her living room, she focused her thoughts on the enjoyable time she had just spent with Teague. No way was she willing to let Brad spoil her evening.

She glanced at the telephone on her end table. Should she call Teague and tell him what happened? She put the idea quickly out of her mind. She would accomplish nothing by worrying him.

Calling Lexie would be even worse. Piper had gone to bed by now, so she didn't want to wake up the little girl. Lexie would lecture Kassia, but she would also worry. Then she would tell Theo, who would tell Teague, who would most likely be hurt Kassia hadn't called him to start with. No, she couldn't call anyone. What would she gain by burdening her friends? Besides, what could anyone do?

Anyone except the neighbor she didn't know at all, that is. She had pleaded to the Lord for help. People who trusted fate would say the neighbor's appearance was a coincidence. Not so long ago she might have thought the same. But since she had been in Teague's company, her viewpoint had changed. How many people who believed in luck would persevere despite a disabling physical injury that followed a job loss? She couldn't imagine drawing strength on an impersonal random force with no thought or meaning. Teague's calmness and strength in the midst of his troubles left her with a new respect for him—and a new awareness of God's love for her.

Kassia had to believe her neighbor didn't just materialize at the moment she needed him because of coincidence or dumb luck. She believed his emergence was God's answer to her silent, desperate prayer.

But what would happen if Brad decided to make an encore appearance? Could she count on her neighbor to arrive on the scene a second time? Or a third, or even a fourth? And even if he did, Kassia didn't want to become dependent on a neighbor who owed her nothing. She wanted to rely on her own resources. She had chosen to live alone in the city. She was bound to abide by the consequences of that decision, whether good or bad.

She shuddered.

Lord, I don't deserve it, but I hope You will please protect me.

After she said her silent prayer, Kassia realized she had made two petitions to God within a few minutes. Not so long ago, she had taken considerable pride in her ability to take care of herself. Now that she had gotten back into the habit of talking to God more often, even though she couldn't see Him, she didn't feel so alone. Suddenly eager for the day to end, she slipped out of her black boots, blue jeans, and red wool sweater and threw on her nightshirt and tucked herself into bed. She would shower in the morning. Closing her eyes, she muttered one of her favorite lines from *Gone with the Wind*, "As Scarlett O'Hara once said, 'Tomorrow is another day.' "

❧

The next day Kassia awoke with unpleasant thoughts of Brad. Once more she prayed the Lord would protect her.

"I'm getting more and more like Teague," she mumbled as she hopped out of bed. Not long ago a thought like that would have disturbed her. Now it seemed as natural as waking up to face the morning.

Heading to the kitchen to brew her first cup of coffee for the day, Kassia thought about how she'd given the daisies to her neighbor, the protector God sent but whose name she didn't know. Insisting he take the flowers also reminded her of Teague—and Lexie. Kassia hoped the man would remember he had been an answer to prayer when he saw the blooms this morning.

She spooned the deeply roasted ground Kona coffee beans into a filter and inhaled the strong aroma. Already in a better mood, Kassia refocused on the earlier part of the previous day, when she was with Teague. She glanced at the DVD of the vintage movie they'd watched. She had left it on the table as a reminder to return it before the rental period expired.

She poured a cup of the hot brew into one of her favorite black china cups. The enticing aroma and anticipation of smooth coffee was one of her favorite daily rituals. She wondered what it would be like to brew a small pot of coffee each morning. To set out two cups. To fill them both with coffee and present one to her waiting husband. Maybe one day. Maybe one day sooner than she once thought. Swallowing, she barely noticed the flavor as she contemplated how much meeting Teague had changed her life. She had never imagined herself as the motherly type, but in helping Teague through his recovery, she discovered she enjoyed having someone else to care about.

Over the weeks, she'd started wishing she could have Teague to herself. Kassia knew she wasn't the only person concerned about him. The kids in his youth group would stop by for chats during the week or linger after the Sunday meetings. Their parents and other adults from the church never let up in bringing food. Even people from his former workplace, including his boss, dropped in with ice cream and magazines. Whenever Teague received a duplicate of the latest computer periodical, he would never let on to his guest.

Kassia wasn't always present during the visits from other people, but when she happened to be there, she was touched by how everyone seemed to care about Teague in a genuine way. The people from his church didn't appear to be merely showing up or meeting an obligation; rather they demonstrated what the minister at Kassia's home church used to call *agape* love.

Kassia thought back to that first Saturday when she showed up with food only to discover Teague's refrigerator was full. She remembered thinking the help would evaporate as people lost interest in the novelty of Teague's setback. Yet as the weeks went by, their care and concern—along with their offerings of food—remained consistent.

She watched how Teague benefited from such a caring community and wondered if her assessment of Christians in general, largely based on her perceptions of her immediate relatives, had been too harsh. Maybe she shouldn't have been judging everyone else by her family's behavior.

"Maybe it's time for me to go back to church," she said aloud, her voice echoing in the small kitchen.

She had driven past a friendly looking church almost every day since she'd rented her apartment. Only recently had she started reading the sign in front for the sermon topics. This week's had looked intriguing: BLACK SHEEP.

"Hmm. That's me, all right. At least, according to everyone in my family." Well, everyone except Grandma. She missed her grandparents now that they had moved to Florida. Far away—too far to be the effective allies they once were.

She knew one thing. Grandma would want her to go to church. And so would Teague. Yet in her heart she felt called to attend that morning—not because of any person, but because of the One who had not forgotten her name.

A verse from the tenth chapter of John's Gospel entered her mind: *"He calls his own sheep by name and leads them out."*

She recalled the parable Jesus told about the lost sheep. She retrieved her Bible from under a stack of dusty books in her bedroom and, returning to the kitchen, hunted until she found the story in Matthew: *"If a man owns a hundred sheep, and one of them wanders away, will he not leave the ninety-nine on the hills and go to look for the one that wandered off? And if he finds it, I tell you the truth, he is happier about that one sheep than about the ninety-nine that did not wander off."*

"I sure am one of those sheep, Lord."

She took another sip of coffee. Funny how long-forgotten Bible verses were returning to her now that her mind was focusing more on her spiritual life and her untended relationship with the Lord. Funny, since she once judged the church to be filled with people playing at being spiritual, working for God's approval and judging harshly those whom they deemed unworthy. She had turned her back on church and never planned to think about her Bible again.

But now God was beckoning to her. First He sent Lexie, her devout best friend, to live with her for a time. Then in Teague He showed her a glimpse of what life could be like with a Christian man. She could only imagine how much richer her relationship would be with Teague once he admitted to her he loved her—and somehow she felt sure he did. At least, she hoped so. And his acknowledgment would free her to confess her love to him.

A glimpse at the apple-shaped kitchen wall clock told her that if she didn't tarry long, she still had enough time to reach the church for the eleven o'clock worship service. She drained her cup, set it on the white countertop, turned off the coffeepot, and rushed to take a shower.

Moments later Kassia stood in the narrow bathtub and let streams of hot water hit her shoulders and run down her back. The steam mist relaxed and warmed her. Sometimes her most brilliant moments of insight came to her while she stood in the middle of her shower. Whether the water's cleansing effects or the steam's ability to clear her head were the reasons, she wasn't sure.

She poured gardenia-scented liquid soap into her palm. As she rubbed her hands together to bring it to a lather, the strong scent came to life. The soap had been a splurge, but by using it with her matching talcum powder and cologne, Kassia smelled like a living gardenia all day.

After cleansing she shut off the water, stepped out of the tub, and dried herself. She grabbed the first decent dress she could find in her closet and wriggled into it. She hoped the long-sleeved black shift with vertical red, white, and gray stripes would look suitable for church. She hadn't darkened the door of a church since Lexie's wedding and hadn't shown her face at a worship service since her obligatory appearance at the Christmas cantata service last December. She wished Teague were available to give her an opinion on her dress.

She rubbed a spot of scented lotion into her hands. Poor Teague. He wouldn't enjoy the privilege of taking a shower until his ankle healed. She sighed. While she never would have wished any harm to come to him if it could have been avoided, she couldn't help but contemplate how Teague's injury had turned out to be an unexpected blessing.

Since he was incapacitated, the physical issues that plagued Kassia's other relationships were largely absent. With him she didn't have to worry about having to fend off men like Brad.

Brad. The image of him made her frown. Her old crush hadn't turned out to be the ideal man she had first thought. So much for appearances. Then again she had obviously disappointed him, too. Kassia knew she had made her interest in Brad obvious to him. Maybe if she had held back and let men express their interest first, she wouldn't have misled anyone, including Brad, into thinking she was offering more physical promises than she wanted to deliver. As it was, they had both misjudged each other by their appearances.

A picture of Teague popped into her head. Any woman would be proud to sit by him in a church pew or anywhere else. His appearance was hardly what anyone—Christian or worldly—would call unattractive. Far from it.

She felt warmth spread over her face. If she were honest with herself, she would have to admit she wished Teague would at least try to kiss her. But her instincts told her he wouldn't want to share his first kiss with her while he was still laid up with his ankle. If a kiss was meant to be, she would have to wait.

twelve

A few days later Kassia pulled up to Teague's house. She no longer had to pause in front of the mailbox to be sure she had the right address. Her car seemed to guide itself to its destination. Since she had been spending so much time with Teague, being at his house had begun to feel more like home than her own apartment.

She jumped out of the car, eager to begin the evening. Her guitar, nestled in its black nylon cover, lay on the backseat. She had put the instrument in the car at the last minute on impulse, and now she wondered if she had made the right decision. She sometimes strummed a few tunes in the privacy of her apartment to relax her and lift her spirits. But Kassia didn't aspire to play in front of large groups and, unlike her sister Deidre, never performed at important occasions such as weddings. So for her to reveal this part of herself to Teague was a major development.

She hoped he wouldn't be disappointed when she showed up at his house without a DVD. Maybe some tunes would lift their spirits this evening instead.

She smiled. Her guitar was a brilliant shade of crimson with silver flecks and looked as if it belonged to someone who played hard rock instead of soft tunes. She wondered what Teague would think of it. But after her unpleasant encounter with Brad, she'd been more jittery the past few days at work, and playing had helped calm her when she was at home alone.

She'd also started doing something even more important—viewing every day as a tapestry, she hemmed each one in prayer. The Lord had answered by keeping Brad out of sight. She was thankful he had gotten the message.

"Hey," she greeted Teague as he answered the door.

"Hey, yourself," he answered.

Knocking hadn't been necessary. Teague was in the habit of watching for her on the nights of her expected arrival and would hobble to the door to greet her.

"Sorry I didn't bring a movie," she said as she stepped over the threshold. "I didn't see anything good."

He nodded toward the guitar she was carrying by a strap on her shoulder. "But I see you brought something else. A guitar?"

She nodded.

"Really?" His eyes brightened. "Why didn't you tell me you played the guitar? We could have used your talent many times at our youth meetings."

She pointed her finger in his direction. "Exactly."

He laughed. "Oh, I get it. You're shy." He made his way over to the chair where he spent most of his time and sat down.

She propped her guitar against the wall by the closet then took off her jacket and found a slot for it among several coats already stuffed into the small space. She wondered why a bachelor needed so many coats. She speculated he never threw his old ones away.

"I admit it," she said. "I'm a little shy about performing in front of other people. I don't even perform in front of my family. My sister Deidre is much better at playing the guitar anyway."

"I doubt that."

"I appreciate your confidence, but she's pretty awesome." Kassia felt envy bubbling to the surface. "I'm just a fair to middling player. That's why it's taken me so long to tell you I can strum a few tunes." She winked. "I figure since I've done your laundry enough times, you'll forgive me if I miss an occasional note."

"I guarantee I'll forgive you." When he smiled from the chair, the warmth of his expression reached across the room and touched her lightly on her cheek, like a kiss. "Okay. I'm ready."

"Now?" Nervousness spiked though her.

"Sure. Why not?"

"Yeah, why not?" She swallowed and walked over to her guitar then picked it up and returned to the living room. If she faced Teague to play, the neck of her instrument would hit the back of the couch. She looked at the brown leather ottoman that matched his other furniture. It was covered with junk mail. "I see you must not be using this much as a footrest."

"It doesn't look like anyone could with all that mess, does it?" He laughed, a pleasant sound that made Kassia want to laugh along with him. "Actually I am. I set my foot on the catalogues to keep my ankle elevated."

"Oh. It's good to know there's some use for all that junk mail."

"Unless you want to sit there," he said. "Then throw that stuff on the floor."

She did so but left the catalogues in a neat pile. "I'll set this back up for you later." Soon she was situated. "So," she asked him, "what do you want me to play? Or try to play, that is?"

He thought for a moment. "Oh, maybe 'Kumbaya'?"

" 'Kumbaya'? Wow!" She recited the tune in her head. "I haven't heard that song in ages, much less played it."

"You don't mind, do you?"

"Of course not. It's easy enough to play. Or at least I can fake it."

Almost every song he suggested was a classic that brought back memories of church camp. Singing them again made her feel wistful—not for the past she experienced but for a past she could never claim. After they sang "Amazing Grace," she stopped for a moment and stared into space.

"What are you thinking about?" Teague asked.

She turned toward him. "Church camp. My sisters and I used to go for a week every summer."

"So you have fond memories of roasting hot dogs and marshmallows over an open fire and singing songs as I do?" He smiled.

Kassia wasn't sure how to answer. Even though they had come to know each other more over the past weeks, she wasn't ready to share the whole truth. Not yet anyway.

She decided to change the subject. "I think I've found a place where I can make new memories in a Christian fellowship."

"You have? Where?"

"At the big brick church near my apartment."

"The Fellowship of the Son?"

Kassia nodded. "That's the one."

"I've always wondered what that church is like. Their building dominates the whole block," Teague said.

"I know. I was surprised to walk in and find the worship being held in a big auditorium that was almost full when I got there—a little late, as usual for me." She grinned. "I visited their service last Sunday, and they were as nice as they could be. The sermon was good, too," she added. "The message was based on the Bible, but it talked about God's love instead of being too scary."

His eyes took on a brighter light than she remembered seeing. "That's great, Kassia. I've been praying you'd find a good church. An experience like that makes you feel as if you're coming home, doesn't it?"

Not exactly. You wouldn't want to come to my home.

Avoiding his question she began to strum her guitar.

❧

After she played "Amazing Grace," Teague noticed that Kassia couldn't seem to regain her momentum. Instead of being happy she had enjoyed a favorable experience in church, she seemed more aloof than ever. Something was bothering her, and that fact left him with more questions than answers. The more he thought he knew Kassia, the more mysterious she became. He wished he could reach into her heart somehow, so he could help with whatever it was that was troubling her. But he couldn't. He had to wait until she was ready to open up to him.

Relax, he told himself. *Just take the moment and enjoy everything.* He thought of one of his favorite verses in the book of Matthew: *"Who of you by worrying can add a single hour to his life?"*

He decided that was good advice from Jesus and only a little bit of His abiding wisdom.

Teague knew he would be wise to relax and enjoy this rest as much as he could. Once his ankle was healed, he would have no more excuses. His savings accounts were running low, and he would need to be aggressive in finding more work. The resumes he had sent out hadn't yielded any offers yet. True to her promise, Mom had driven him to the one interview he was offered; but Teague could see the job wasn't a good fit for him, and the stiff body language of the interviewer told him the feeling had been mutual. He hadn't been surprised when no second interview materialized.

Teague refused to be depressed or tell anyone that at times he felt defeated. Not that he put on a false front when someone asked about his prospects. Being a hypocrite wouldn't accomplish anything or encourage anyone. By keeping his focus on healing, he would be up and about faster and able to pursue his options full force and without crutches.

In the meantime he had resolved to enjoy Kassia's attention. He had been praying she would see the Christian community in action as a result of his mishap, and he wasn't disappointed. In their conversations she was less closed to talking about God and Christianity. Her comments were growing more positive. And he could sense her relationship with the Lord was becoming more important to her.

The fact made him comfortable about opening up to her. Not that he could have avoided it completely. She had seen him looking—and feeling—his worst. Yet she still kept visiting. Only weeks ago he couldn't have imagined wanting a woman to come over almost every day and prepare him meals and be with him for hours at a time. Yet somehow Kassia never smothered him. If only he had something more to offer her than a chance to play nursemaid. But he didn't. Not yet. He had been surprised she hadn't run away once she found out he had no job and no immediate prospects of one. She must have been coming over because she felt sorry for him. The fact that a friendship had developed gave him hope.

But was he falling in love with her? No. He just felt helpless, that's all. The emotions, his heart beating faster when he heard her car pull up in his driveway, his breath catching when he saw her, were all signs of gratitude. Or were they?

❧

Kassia was about to head out of her apartment to run a few errands when she heard a knock on her apartment door. Her stomach lurched.

Please don't let it be Brad.

She looked through the peephole and saw a familiar blond woman. "Whew!" Kassia opened the door.

"Hey!" Lexie wore the beaming smile of a happy honeymooner. "I hope you don't mind that I stopped by. I was on my way to check out the new health food store and realized I was driving right by here. I couldn't resist seeing if you were home." She looked beyond Kassia to the coffee table where Kassia's keys and purse sat on top of the inevitable pile of papers and magazines. "Were you on your way out? I can stop by another time."

"No! No! Not at all!" Kassia's voice sounded as bright as she felt. "Come on in. I'd much rather see you than run all over town. And the dry cleaner and drugstore are open all day anyway."

Lexie stepped inside. "Do you want to check out the new health food store with me after we visit awhile?"

"Sure, but I've already been."

"Is it any good?"

"I bought a few things the last time I went." Kassia realized someone was missing. "I notice you left Piper at home. She could have picked out some organic cereals and cookies."

"I hadn't thought of that. I just didn't want to listen to her beg to go to the dollar store next door." Lexie grinned. "So they have cereal and cookies? Wow! Wonder what makes them organic?"

"The ingredients in the cereals and cookies are grown without chemicals or pesticides."

"Oh." She shook her head. "They have thought way beyond me."

Kassia laughed. "If you'll come on in the kitchen with me, I'll make you some tea."

"Organic?"

"Sorry, no," Kassia confessed. "Maybe next time."

"I think I'll live."

Kassia walked ahead, and Lexie followed her. Even though Lexie had once lived with her, she cringed when she noticed she had neglected to dust and the carpet needed a good vacuuming. "Sorry the place is such a mess. I haven't been here much."

"So I've heard." Lexie pulled out a wooden chair and sat down at the matching knotty pine table.

"What do you mean?" Kassia asked, though she could guess. She took a box of tea bags out of the cabinet. A faint odor of sweet spices greeted her.

"Teague told Theo you've been taking good care of him since he got injured."

Kassia felt her face grow warm. "Did he?" She poured fresh water into the teakettle.

"Yes, and I'm very proud of you."

Kassia turned on the stove to heat the water. "Proud of me?"

"Yes. For being so faithful to Teague, even when you hardly know him at all. Unless there's something you're not telling me."

Kassia sat in another chair at the table while the water heated. She swept aside a pile of unanswered mail and mail-order catalogues cluttering the table. "No, I didn't know him very well when the accident happened. But I've had a chance to learn a lot about him since then."

"Ah. The proverbial silver lining."

"I wouldn't have willed such an accident to happen to Teague for all the silver in the world."

"Then it must be love." Lexie winked at her friend.

"Oh, stop it. Don't be ridiculous." Yet Kassia could sense her face was getting hotter.

"Oh, stop it yourself. You can barely stand it because you're so in love with him." Lexie's tone was light, but Kassia could see she wasn't kidding. "And if Theo is telling me the truth, Teague feels the same way, whether he knows it or not."

Kassia warmed with pleasure; then she felt chills of uncertainty. It was one thing to fantasize about Teague and think about how much she liked being with him. Yet Lexie telling her she and Teague were being talked about as a couple was quite another.

"You exaggerate," Kassia protested. "You know what a vivid imagination Theo has."

"Maybe so. But he's a good judge of what Teague is thinking. They've been friends since they were in college," Lexie pointed out. "He told me Teague couldn't stop talking about you the whole time they were together."

The teapot whistled, and Kassia left her seat to tend to it. "I wish you had brought Piper." She drew her black china cups and saucers from the cabinet. She always enjoyed using the octagonal-shaped dishes.

"Why is that?"

Kassia poured hot water into the cups and dropped a tea bag in each. "She would have told you to stop speaking such nonsense."

"That's what you think. Remember—she still doesn't mind having boys as playmates."

"She'll start thinking they have cooties soon enough." Kassia set the cups on the table and returned to her seat.

"Then she'll start liking them again," Lexie mused.

"All too soon." Kassia sighed then swirled the tea bag in her cup.

"All too soon," Lexie echoed and sighed. She smiled faintly.

"Be sure to tell her I missed seeing her."

"I'll have to bring her over sometime for a visit." Lexie glanced at her watch. "She has a tumbling lesson in a few minutes so I couldn't have brought her anyway. Theo's pulling duty today. They must be getting in the car to leave for the gym right about now."

"You're so lucky they've taken to each other so well," Kassia said, a wistful tone in her voice.

"You know I don't attribute anything that important to an uncaring, random force like luck," Lexie said.

"I know." Kassia braced herself for a sermon.

"But you are right about one thing. It's not every day you find a guy who's willing to take a package deal like us and with such a loving spirit. And speaking of packages, I didn't bring Piper for another reason. She doesn't know yet." She stared into the cup as though she were planning to read tea leaves instead of drink the hot liquid.

"Know what?" Kassia asked.

"Our package is about to get bigger."

Kassia furrowed her brows. "Huh? Speak English."

"Okay." Lexie didn't lift her gaze from the cup. "I'm expecting." Her face turned as pink as a young bride's.

"Expecting? Wow! Already?" Kassia blurted out.

"I know." Lexie laughed, the corners of her eyes crinkling with joy. "I must have conceived on my wedding night."

"Do you mind that it's so soon?" Kassia asked.

Lexie shook her head and smiled. "Not at all. It's about time Piper had a little brother or sister. I can't believe she'll be six on her next birthday."

"She's growing up fast. I'm so happy for you." Kassia leaned over and hugged her friend. "When are you going to tell her?"

"Maybe in a couple of months. I want to make sure I'm showing first."

"I'm sure she'll notice as soon as you gain the first pound," Kassia observed. "Nothing gets past her."

Kassia smiled and hoped her expression looked convincing. Truly she was happy for her friend, but Lexie's good news only reminded her that her own life wasn't nearly as full.

☙

That evening, after she had spent a few hours shopping with Lexie and running errands around town, Kassia was ready to drop in front of the television and relax. Yet as she flipped through the channels and saw nothing appealing, she grew even more restless. She turned off the television, leaving the room silent. Despite her happiness for her friend, Kassia had bitten back envy at Lexie's rich family life. Her husband was loving and supportive, her little girl was adorable, and her parents and extended family members were always there for her. Plus the anticipation of a new life would only increase her happiness. Lexie never boasted or threw her joy in Kassia's face. On the contrary, she celebrated every victory of Kassia's with her. But Lexie didn't need to say a word about her fantastic life. Radiance exuded from her.

"Why can't it be like that for me?" she asked an invisible audience.

In her heart, Kassia knew the answer. She realized she had something much more important to do than stare at the television. No amount of stalling would change that.

She shivered with fear and wonder as images of the prodigal son popped into her head. Kassia recalled another time and place, a time of innocence, when she fully trusted God. Before she entered her teen years and began to resent her parents' heavy involvement in their church activities. Before she seethed with rage at being thrust into the church youth group. Before she found a new group of friends, with attitudes about life that were different from the ones she knew. Before she rebelled.

She reached for the phone. Maybe it was time to talk to her parents. Not just a conversation where she would share the latest news with her mother and receive a lecture, but a real, two-way exchange. Maybe even face-to-face. At present they lived three hours away by car, and she hadn't seen them since Christmas. And now she was going to change that.

She drummed the receiver with her fingers, hesitating. If she wanted a right relationship with God, though, she knew she needed to make her relationship right, or as right as it could be, with her parents.

"With God all things are possible." In minutes she would be testing that verse for herself.

thirteen

The next week, Kassia was glad for Teague's company as she drove to see her parents. Even though he still had a few more days left before his walking cast would be removed, he had agreed to go with her. She could see by the way he observed the passing scenery that he was glad to be out in the world.

The season lifted Kassia's spirits. Spring, a time of rebirth, renewal and new beginnings, always filled her with optimism. Large trees were budding, with fresh green leaves about to pop out so each would soon bear its unique umbrella of glory. The more ambitious flowering trees and shrubs already provided their own contribution to the picture.

Kassia rolled down her window. Pleasant air with a slight chill entered the car.

She thought about her traveling companion. "You don't mind the air, do you?"

"No," Teague answered. "I was about to ask if I could roll down my window."

Even though the breeze brought with it the smell of exhaust fumes, she could still breathe in the light aroma of the season. The highway department had apparently just mowed, for newly cut grass in the median emitted a crisp scent. The fragrance of flowers blooming alongside the road softened the atmosphere. She thought back to her neighbor's reference to Mother Nature and could understand why some people might look at the world as the work of a random force. But God, the Alpha and the Omega, encompassed all aspects of heaven and earth. Kassia was no longer willing to give one iota of credit for this creation to anyone other than Jehovah Himself.

She could only hope her family would sense the change in her and offer their welcome.

"What are you thinking about?" Teague asked.

"Oh, nothing." Guilt shot through her. She needed to let him know. The time had come. "Well, okay. I am thinking about something," she admitted. "A lot of somethings. Things that maybe I should have told you about when I asked you to come along with me today." She glanced at him then returned her attention to the road.

She could see him staring at the road with as much intensity as if he were driving the car instead of her.

"Well," he finally ventured, "I get the feeling you aren't close to your family. If I remember correctly, you may have even mentioned it at some point."

"Unfortunately you're right. We don't get along too well."

"I wondered if you were bringing me along as reinforcement."

She gulped. Was she really so transparent? "Maybe there was a little bit of that. I know they'll be on their best behavior in front of you."

The giggle that escaped her lips was more nervous than happy. She had another reason for wanting him to come along on the trip. For better or worse, she wanted Teague to meet her family. Her time of nursing him along as he recovered from his surgery was drawing to a close. He would soon be able to move around freely, and he had already told her he'd be pursuing a new job with all his energy. His time for her would be more limited, and with so many excuses, she could easily evaporate from his life.

She didn't want that to happen. She wanted to be there for him as a friend—maybe more. Okay, definitely more. To be fair to Teague, she wanted him to see what her family was like before he pursued her any further, if he decided to do so. And she hoped her invitation would show him her interest in him extended beyond sympathy.

"I'm sure we'll get along great."

"I hope so, since you can't run out of the house too fast." She laughed then became serious. "Teague, I guess you know I've been trying to learn more about the real meaning of salvation—and the Lord's plan for my life—since you and I met.

He reached his hand over and laid it on her shoulder. "Yes, and I'm proud of you for that. I can see you've come a long way in a short time."

"Thanks, but I still have a long way to go. Part of the process for me is to try to get on better terms with my parents and sisters. I know it won't happen overnight, but I'm hoping to start today, at least with my parents and older sister, Deidre. My little sister, Mona, won't be there."

"You said her college has midterms scheduled this week."

"You remembered."

"Sure. Why wouldn't I remember what you say?" he asked.

"Don't most women complain that men don't listen to them?"

"You're not most women."

"And obviously you're not most men." She glanced at him and smiled.

"I hope that's a good thing." He smiled, too.

"I do believe it is."

❧

Kassia was nervous as she stepped out of the car. She paused by the open side door and regarded her childhood home. The two-story brick Georgian-style house that had once seemed so large appeared modest to her adult eyes. The side yard where she had spent hours running and playing had changed. An ancient oak tree had been replaced with green boxwood and azalea shrubs starting to show promise of brilliant blooms.

Teague's head popped up over the roof of the car. "Nice place."

"It used to be home." Her voice quivered.

"Are you ready?" Teague asked.

Kassia nodded and shut the door.

She walked around the car, and Teague hobbled up beside her. "Don't try to heal old wounds too fast," he said in a low voice. "Just treat this like any other visit. The reconciliation will come in time."

Teague's wisdom and assurance strengthened her, along with a silent prayer that all would go well.

She noticed him heading for the side door. "No. This way."

He stopped and gave her a quizzical look. "We're going to the front door?"

She clenched her teeth. "Mother is a bit formal. She wouldn't want anyone entering the house through the side door."

"Oh." Teague complied, but his puzzled look remained.

Soon they were standing on the front stoop. Kassia lifted the heavy brass door knocker, shaped into the head of a lion, and let it drop. The familiar *thud* of metal on metal sounded like home, though the thought occurred to her that other families might have run out in the yard to greet their daughter and sister rather than waiting for her to knock on the door.

After some time had passed without a response, Kassia glanced at her watch. "We're right on time, at least by my watch. I have no idea why they're taking so long."

"Try again. Maybe they didn't hear you."

She nodded in outward agreement, but her heart told her the delayed greeting was a preview of coming attractions.

Before she could lift the knocker a second time, Mother opened the door. "Kassia. You're here." Her thin lips barely moved as she spoke.

"Yes, ma'am," she answered. "We're on time, I hope."

"You're only a few minutes late. But we're used to you by now, Kassia." Her mother gave her an embrace that managed to be cold. She never had been touchy-feely, least of all with Kassia.

Mother raked her gaze over Teague as though he were a

distasteful object she was being forced to examine before discarding. "And this is your friend?"

"Yes, ma'am," he piped up with more cheerfulness than Kassia could have mustered. "Teague Boswell." He leaned his weight on one crutch then awkwardly extended the other hand in greeting. Kassia doubted her mother welcomed the gesture, but she shook his hand stiffly nevertheless.

"Come in," Mother said, as though the invitation was necessary, and turned for them to follow her. "Deidre and your father are in the living room. I'll be serving lunch at noon." She disappeared through the doorway.

Kassia knew her mother would keep her word. Her life was one of productivity, punctuality, and order. As usual, the house looked as though the rooms were ready for a photographer to enter any moment. Her mother could never abide clutter. Deidre and Mona happily became neatniks themselves. Kassia, without meaning to, always frustrated her mother with her mellow attitude toward time and her indifference to housework. At least they weren't meeting in her apartment. No matter how much she cleaned, Kassia could never live up to her mother's standards.

Quickly Kassia made the introductions and was pleased her prediction about her family being on their best behavior was true. At least, as good as they could be. Kassia felt grateful when her father seemed to take a genuine liking to Teague. She knew she had cleared the first hurdle when he took Teague into his study to see his collection of Native American fetish stones, small figurines of animals carved out of rock.

Their absence left Kassia alone with her older sister. Deidre was expecting her second child, but she didn't let the extra weight stop her from looking her best.

"Nice haircut," Kassia noticed.

"Oh, thanks." Deidre touched her shorn locks, which were flipped upward. "I think this makes me look more friendly and flatters my face."

Kassia noticed Deidre hadn't abandoned her bangs, a styling trick she had used for years to cover a scar she acquired from a long-ago fall from the swing set. "That style is very attractive on you," she agreed.

As the strong midday sun shone on her sister's face, Kassia noticed Deidre was wearing a thick coat of her usual foundation. For the most part, she had succeeded in covering the ravages acne had left. Kassia was attentive to her own appearance but not vain. She knew Deidre had long believed she wasn't as pretty as Kassia and that those feelings contributed to her cold attitude.

"I had scheduled an open house today," Deidre said, referring to her work as a real-estate agent, "but as soon as Mother said you'd be visiting, I decided to let my assistant handle it."

"I'm sorry I caused you to change your plans." Kassia bit her lip. Why did she always feel the need to apologize to her sister?

Deidre sat on the edge of the couch striped in green and beige as though it were a throne rather than a modest sofa. The knobby material blended well with textured beige wallpaper Mother had recently installed herself. Kassia's sister clasped her hands over her knees. "I suppose she has to learn how to conduct an open house sometime. That sometime might as well be now."

"I understand you're selling quite a few houses."

"Yes. I'm the top seller in my office, although I do try to leave as much time open as I can for the family. Can't let the marriage wilt for lack of nurturing, you know." Deidre leaned forward as though she were about to take her into her confidence. "The only reason I had scheduled the open house for today was because Matt wanted to take little Tyler camping. That's why they're not here, by the way. Matt sends his regrets."

"I'm sorry I won't be able to see them, especially Tyler. I brought him a present. A toy truck."

"Matt's parents just gave him a truck, but I'm sure yours will be fine."

Kassia struggled not to grimace. No gift would have pleased Deidre unconditionally.

"We so often prefer to buy him educational toys," Deidre stated. "Tyler is quite the prodigy, you know. No doubt he'll be able to identify every species of flora and fauna on his return."

"No doubt." Kassia held back a sigh and painted a smile on her face.

"They'll be back in time for the dinner at church tonight. Our women's group is putting on a talent show to raise money for missions."

"That sounds noble. I hope you succeed," Kassia said in all sincerity.

"How are things at your church?" Deidre raised her eyebrows.

"Great. I've been attending a church with a lovely Christian fellowship near my apartment. You'll have to go with me the next time you visit."

"Oh!" Deidre leaned back suddenly. "Well. That's nice." She still seemed to doubt Kassia's sincerity. At least Teague wasn't in the room to see how small her sister could make her look—and feel.

Deidre glanced at the doorway leading from the living room into the hall. "There you are, Teague. I hope Father didn't bore you to death with his collection."

"Not at all. I learned a lot." Teague made his way slowly to the chair beside Kassia. She knew from experience the chair looked more comfortable than it was.

"I was telling Teague how our church funded a mission program to the Native Americans years ago, and that's what inspired me to collect the figurines," Father said as he took a seat on the couch next to Deidre. "Only for amusement, of course."

Deidre touched her father's shoulder. "That was a wonderful mission trip. Remember what a great time we had in Arizona?" Deidre launched into a series of stories that were part of their family lore. Family lore for everyone but Kassia. She had studied in Europe that summer.

"So, Kassia, we're so glad we finally get to meet Teague," Deidre said. "I do hope it wasn't too much for you to come all this way with that cast still on." She looked at Teague's ankle as though it offended her.

"I'm fine, thanks."

"Lucky you, for being able to take off so much time from work. My boss would have my head on a platter if I tried to pull such a stunt." Deidre's laugh was hollow. "So what do you do for a living, Teague?"

Kassia rushed to answer for him. "Teague is in software development."

"Well, I was," Teague said. "Right now I'm looking for a job."

Kassia groaned inwardly. All she needed was for Deidre to know Teague was unemployed. Now her whole family would think he was a bum. Deidre's raised eyebrows only confirmed Kassia's suspicions.

"Oh, really?" Deidre said. "Kassia never said anything about your bad luck. I'm so sorry. I would certainly be worried if I lost my job in this economy. I hope you can find something else soon. Do you have any good prospects?"

"I sent out a bunch of resumes, and I've had one job interview, but that didn't work out. I hope someone will respond favorably soon. I have to say this ankle has slowed me down. When I get the cast off next week, I plan to broaden my search." In spite of his brave assurances, Teague's face clouded for the first time that day. Apparently he found Deidre's probing questions discouraging.

Kassia attempted to come to his rescue. "Teague will find something else soon. He is extremely talented at what he does. You know what? His pet project is one you'll want Tyler to play when he gets older—a Christian computer game."

"Oh." For one sweet moment, Kassia had shut her sister's mouth.

Deidre recovered quickly. "We're so lucky. Matt has never been unemployed a day in his life."

"It doesn't hurt that Matt works for his dad," Kassia couldn't resist pointing out. Ignoring her father's knowing smile and her sister's harsh expression toward her, Kassia broached another topic. "Father, did Teague tell you he's a youth leader at his church?"

"No, but you mentioned it when you told us about his accident." The older man turned to Teague. "That's the reason you got in trouble with your ankle, isn't it?"

"I was on a trip with the youth," Teague admitted. "But I can't blame the kids for my accident."

Kassia cringed. "It was just an unfortunate accident," she told her father. "I saw it happen. His ski hit a rock or something else hidden under the snow on the trail."

At that moment, Mother summoned the family to the dining room. Kassia couldn't remember a time when the prospect of lunch was more welcome.

Kassia wasn't surprised to discover her mother had prepared her best meal for them. Deidre and Kassia would have helped her, but Mother always wanted the kitchen to herself. The roast beef and several fancy accompaniments proved her prowess in the kitchen. She basked in the compliments she received.

As soon as he finished a generous slice of apple pie, Father turned to Teague. "Why don't you come on into the study where you can sit awhile? We can watch the baseball game."

Kassia knew she could trust Dad not to be too hard on Teague. She nodded gratefully. "Is that okay with you, Teague? If you need to get home—"

"No, I want to watch the game with your dad." She knew him well enough by now to realize the way he grinned at her meant he was sincere.

"Come on into the kitchen with us," her mother told her.

Since her family knew Kassia was not a baseball fan, she couldn't beg off and escape to the study with the men. She gave Teague a weak grin and headed toward the kitchen.

Situated in the back of the house, the kitchen was the picture-perfect image of modern technology and hygiene. Mother always cleaned up after each meal. No dish was allowed to remain dirty for more than fifteen minutes. Nary a crumb was missed by the ever-moving sponge.

Deidre peered out of the kitchen window toward the driveway. "It's a wonder that rattletrap car of yours made it here."

Since Kassia had resolved to be conciliatory and had already used up her snide quotient on the remark about Matt's working for his dad, she was determined not to take the bait this time. "I know it isn't new like yours, but it does okay."

As Kassia and her mother sat down at the table, Deidre wasted no time in cutting her sister a slice of cake. "Here. Try this. It's my newest recipe."

"Deidre always was the best cook among us," Mother said.

"I know, Mother, but I'm full right now. I just had a big slice of your delicious pie. May I have some cake later?"

"It will be gone if you wait," Mother insisted. "Maybe you should take Teague a slice of your cake, Deidre."

"I can ask him if he'd like to try some." Kassia welcomed the opportunity to escape and check on Teague. She carried a plate with several slices of cake on it and some napkins to the study.

"How are you two doing in here?"

"Great. The game's pretty close," Teague said, smiling at her.

"Deidre wants everyone to try this cake she made. She said it's a new recipe."

Teague took a slice. "Thanks. There's nothing like a great meal followed by two desserts."

"It's delicious," Father said after taking a bite. "Deidre's a great cook. Not that our Kassia isn't. . . ."

"Oh, I know she is. She's been making meals for me since I've been laid up with this ankle."

Father's eyes widened. "Is that so?"

"I come over in the evening after work and stay a couple of hours," Kassia hastened to explain.

"Oh. Then good for you, Kassia. I'm glad you learned some compassion before you left this house." She noticed a glimmer of approval she hadn't seen in years.

Kassia left before they could make any more observations. *I'm not just being a Good Samaritan, Father.*

"So," Mother said when Kassia returned to the kitchen, "Deidre tells me you're going to church now."

"True. I think I've found a good place."

"Do they have a good women's circle there?" Deidre inquired.

"Uh, I don't know."

"Well, you certainly should make it your business to find out!" Mother said sharply. "Deidre just got elected the head of the entire women's group at our church."

Kassia put on her most congratulatory smile. "Good for you."

She listened to the litany of accomplishments in a like vein until her mother and sister exhausted their repertoire. She praised their deeds and recognitions, knowing in their opinion hers would never measure up to theirs. As usual, Kassia felt like a failure next to the golden daughters, even absent Mona. Her sisters were perfect in all their roles, doing their parents proud. Again Kassia was reminded she was the black sheep.

As her mother and her sister talked, Kassia looked around the kitchen. The spotless room symbolized everything her mother was: orderly, formal, hardworking, and practical. They were so different; no wonder her mother didn't understand Kassia. No wonder everything about Kassia frustrated her. If she was determined to change her part in the script, she had to realize the others had worked hard to hone their roles. They weren't going to change, and as far as they were concerned, they had no reason to change. If she wanted a better relationship, she had to be the one who was willing to meet them halfway. Maybe even more than halfway.

"I'll bet you think I only visited to introduce you to Teague," she ventured when they finally ran out of wind.

"The thought did occur to us," Mother said.

"So it's serious?" Deidre asked. "I'd be worried if he's unemployed."

"You've already made that clear, thank you."

Deidre lifted her hands toward Kassia. "Okay. Don't listen. But I've been married long enough to know how much a stable income means."

"I know. And you do have a point." She swallowed. "Thanks for caring enough to mention it."

Time and time again.

Deidre's puzzled look told Kassia she sensed their family dynamics were changing somehow.

Kassia decided to move on before she lost her nerve. She cleared her throat. "Anyway, I came here today for another reason." Kassia studied an embroidered flower on the white tablecloth and said a quick silent prayer. After she finally gathered enough courage to look them in the eye, she spoke. "I want to renew my relationship with God—and with you."

"Really?" Deidre cast a doubtful look toward Mother.

"Really." Kassia's voice was firm. "I don't know what I'll have to do to prove it."

"You don't have to prove anything to us," Mother said. "Just the fact that you came here today is a start."

Kassia nodded. For the first time, she realized her mother was unaware of the fact that she felt inferior around her and her sisters.

"You've said things like this before," Deidre said. "And you've always ended up falling away."

"Not too far, though," Mother pointed out. She reached for Kassia's hands and took them in hers. "Thank you."

"Um, yeah," Deidre muttered.

Despite her mother's kindness, her sister's doubt made Kassia feel worse. But she had always known any relationship with more than twenty-five years of wounds wouldn't be healed in five minutes.

She rose from her chair and motioned to her mother and sister. "Okay. Enough of this seriousness. Let's see how Dad and Teague are doing in the other room."

Deidre was the first to enter the study, a room that still bore paneled walls from another era. The study was the only place in the house that was off-limits to Mother's decorating whims.

"Who's winning?" Deidre asked.

"It's tied."

"Hmm," Kassia noted. "Sounds like a good game."

"A bit slow, really," Teague said. "Your father's been giving me some job-hunting tips, though." He threw Kassia a look that pleaded for a quick rescue.

"I suggested he look for something else instead of traipsing all over the state."

Kassia tried not to cringe. Father meant well, but she felt certain Teague didn't ride all this way with her just to listen to advice. She strode over to Father's old recliner, where he sat like a medieval ruler, and kissed him on the forehead. "Thanks, Father. Teague's talented. He'll find something else soon. And he's sent out a lot of resumes."

"In this economy, you can't try hard enough," her father pointed out.

"Always the optimist," Kassia said.

"Remember Bruce?" Mother asked. "He didn't have a job either, did he, Kassia?"

Kassia groaned at the mention of an old flame. "That was a long time ago."

"He was a troublemaker, as far as I can remember," Father added.

"And Justin wasn't much better."

"Now you're really reaching," Kassia objected.

Teague shot Kassia a look that was both questioning and sympathetic.

Grateful for his unspoken understanding, Kassia rolled her eyes at him and shook her head.

"I hope you're not like the rest of her boyfriends," Mother observed.

"Mother!" Kassia moaned.

"I don't know about her past boyfriends, but I do know your daughter has been good to me since the accident." Teague grinned shyly at the family.

"Well, I'm glad she's finally found some missionary zeal," Mother said. "Maybe you've brought it out in her. We certainly never succeeded."

With Teague's silent approval, Kassia managed to steer them both out of the house before much more could be said. From the perspective of making Teague feel comfortable, the visit had been a total failure. Kassia tried not to let her distress show on her face. If Teague was even willing to speak to her after such a day, she would consider herself blessed.

fourteen

As soon as they were in the car, Kassia turned on the radio. Since they had shared pleasant conversation on the way to her parents' house, Teague suspected her interest in music could be attributed to a sudden disinterest in talking.

Not that he blamed her. Finally Teague could understand why Kassia had always seemed so mysterious. Her family relationship was strained, at best. He had suspected her past failures were a result of misguided searches for love and acceptance. She was a woman in need of both. The question he needed to contemplate—was he the man to love her and accept her as more than a friend?

Looking over at her as she drove up the highway, he believed he was. Yet he knew his feelings were based partly on gratitude. She hardly knew him, and yet she had selflessly spent time with him and cared for him throughout his recovery. She had earned a friend for life—that much was certain. But to base anything stronger on gratitude was a mistake he didn't want to make.

"It's not too late," Kassia noted as they reached the city limits. "Would you like to stop by my apartment for a bite of supper? It's the least I can do."

Teague was hungry, and the idea sounded tempting. "Sure."

"I can make spaghetti if you like."

"Sounds like that will hit the spot."

Not long afterward, Teague and Kassia were sitting comfortably at her dining room table, enjoying the pasta and red sauce.

"Look," she said. "I'm sorry for the way my family acted

while we were there. You can see why I don't visit much. I'm a disappointment to them."

"I don't see why you're a disappointment. They should be proud of you."

"Really?" Kassia's tone indicated she didn't believe him. "Look at Deidre. She's married to a great Christian guy, and she's expecting her second child. Mona is on the dean's list at college and holds an office in practically every club she's in—and she's a member of almost everything on campus except the fraternities. And she'd join those if they were allowed to take her."

Teague chuckled.

"You can laugh, but it's not much fun when you're a sibling of a superstar." She sighed. "It's always been that way. I've been literally in the middle in both age and achievements. I've never been a standout in anything. How can I compete with them?"

"Who says you have to compete?"

She twirled a clump of noodles around her fork with more vigor than necessary. "I don't. I gave up trying a long time ago."

"But you still resent their success."

"Not really. I want to be happy for them." She opened her mouth as if to add something, when they heard a knock on the door. "I'd better see who that is. Excuse me. I'll be right back."

Not wanting to be a busybody, Teague remained at the table. Yet in the small apartment he could easily overhear the conversation.

"I left a message on your desk Friday that I'd be by at lunchtime today. Didn't you get it?"

"I got it."

"Then where were you?" The caller's tone indicated disgust and something else—was it ownership?

Teague wondered who would dare speak to Kassia that way. He felt the muscles tighten in his face. The voice sounded familiar. Who was it?

"I was out." Kassia didn't sound like the sweet woman he knew.

"Where?"

"None of your business," Kassia snapped.

"You were with him, weren't you?"

Teague still couldn't identify the man without seeing him. Whoever he was, he was no friend of Kassia's. Since the distance was short, he left his crutches leaning against the table and limped into the next room.

"Who I'm with is none of your business," Kassia was saying.

Teague spotted a tall, dark-haired man standing in Kassia's doorway. Brad! What was he doing here?

"Is that you, Teak?" Brad's eyes narrowed. "No, don't answer that. It's just what I thought."

"And what did you think?" Teague wanted to know.

"That you've been pushing yourself on her, even though you knew Kassia and I were seeing each other."

"Seeing each other?" Teague wondered aloud.

"That's not true," Kassia said. "Brad and I went on a couple of dates, and that's it. He wanted nothing to do with me until he saw us together in the restaurant that night, Teague. Now he won't leave me alone. He's been harassing me ever since."

"That's not so," Brad objected. "Kassia chased me for months before I took any notice of her. Now she claims she doesn't want to see me. How do you like that?"

"What do you mean, she chased you?" Teague asked.

"We work in the same office complex. She had her eye on me for months."

"And you, like some kind of king or something, decided to grant her the honor of your notice?" Teague scoffed.

Brad folded his arms.

"Your highness, I'm afraid your subject Kassia has changed her mind. She no longer wishes to see you. Isn't that right, Kassia?"

"Yes, it is. I've been trying to get rid of him for weeks. I came home one night and found him waiting here in front of my door. I told him to leave then, but obviously he didn't listen," Kassia explained.

"So this isn't the first time he's bothered you." Teague wanted to be sure he had his facts straight.

"That's right." Kassia looked at Brad with an unwavering gaze. "I was so upset the other night when you started an argument with me in the hallway that I prayed to the Lord, and He sent a neighbor to protect me."

"Say what?" Brad asked.

Teague didn't have to question Kassia. He knew exactly what she meant. He put on his toughest expression and looked squarely at Brad. "I suggest you leave her alone."

Brad nodded at Teague's cast. "And I guess you think you're going to make me?" He scowled. "I knew Kassia long before you did. You have no business interfering with us. I suggest you take your little helpless act and find another nurse."

"He is not helpless or putting on an act. It's time for you to leave, Brad, and I mean it when I say I don't want to see you."

"I don't believe you. Do you know how many women in the office would love to be in your shoes right now?"

"Then why don't you take your pick?" Kassia suggested.

"Because I told you I want to be with you. I think he's the one who'll be leaving." He let his stare rove over Kassia. "Kassia and I want to be alone."

Teague felt blood rise from the pit of his belly to the roots of the hair on his head. He looked at Kassia. She was hovering in the nearest corner, watching with her eyes widened in obvious fear.

"I don't think Kassia wants to be alone with you," Teague said.

"That's what you think."

"That's what I know," Teague said. "Didn't you hear the

lady? You even have her petitioning the Lord to help her get away from you."

"Then she's crazier than I thought." Brad narrowed his eyes and hunched toward Teague.

His temper rising, Teague said, "You'd better watch your step, or I'll let you have it." He balled his hand into a fist.

"You just try it, and I'll sue you. I can get you on assault and battery."

"Go ahead. But no jury will be sympathetic toward a common stalker."

"A—a stalker?"

"Yes. From what Kassia has said, that's exactly what you are. There are new laws on the books to deal with people like you. I wouldn't take my chances in court if I were in your place."

Brad looked at Kassia. Teague looked at her, too. She appeared stronger, as if she wouldn't back down.

"All right. I'll go. You can have her and her crazy God stuff." Brad nearly spit out the words before he retreated down the hall.

Kassia closed the door. She ran to Teague and embraced him. "Thank you!"

He had never tried to take advantage of Kassia's sweet nature by asking for a hug. But finally she was in his arms! And they felt so right together. He cupped her face in his hands. Gazing up into his eyes, she looked like a scared little girl. But she seemed to relax after a moment.

"Why didn't you tell me before that he was bothering you?"

"You had enough on your mind with the youth group, and the accident, and then the surgery, and now your recovery. Speaking of which"—she took his hands in hers and broke away—"are you okay? I mean, all this might be too much."

"I'm fine." He wished she could stay in his arms forever.

"You're a hero in my book, but I feel awful I got you involved in my problems. I'm not your responsibility."

"Really? That's what I've been telling you about me. We've proven we wanted to be responsible for each other, haven't we?" He took her hands in his and squeezed them.

She nodded. "It's not such a bad feeling. I'll try not to get in trouble anymore. I have to admit I sort of asked for this. Brad was right. I did chase him around the office until he finally noticed me. And I found out he wasn't all I thought he was."

"They say you can't judge a book by its cover. That's not an easy lesson for any of us to learn."

"I think I learned it this time." She looked at the closed door. "Maybe now he'll finally realize I really, really don't want to see him again." She turned to Teague, and together they went back to the kitchen.

"I hope so. I don't know what else we could do to convince him. And I hope you don't think I get angry like that often. It's not as if Christianity teaches us to lose control of our tempers."

"Yes, I remember. Jesus said the Old Testament taught 'an eye for an eye,' but He told us to forgive one another."

A sense of guilt pierced him. "I never would have lost my cool if—" He stared down at his glass of skim milk where it sat on the table.

"If what?"

"If I didn't have deep feelings for you. Feelings beyond friendship. Maybe, maybe even—" He stopped and looked into Kassia's eyes.

She smiled. "Maybe even what?"

"Well, uh. . ." Teague hesitated.

"You weren't afraid of Brad," Kassia said, smiling. "Don't tell me you're afraid of, well, of love."

"No, I'm not afraid of love," he blurted out finally. "At least I don't think so. Are you?"

"No. For the first time since I can remember, I'm not."

Teague reached over and drew her toward him, stroking the back of her head until his fingers became tangled in her curls.

She didn't pull away when he lowered his face to hers and their lips met. The warm tingle shooting up his spine was nothing like he had felt before. Her body tensed for an instant then conformed to his embrace. Perhaps she wanted this, too, maybe as much as he did!

Suddenly Teague felt scared of his feelings. If Kassia returned them, then what did it mean for him—for them? He released her without warning and stepped away.

"I'd better go. It's getting late. Will you drive me home now?"

"Uh, sure. Don't you want any more dinner?"

"Not now, even though it was very good. After everything that's happened in the last half hour, I don't think I can eat another thing."

&

After she returned home from dropping off Teague at his house, Kassia's feelings churned in a million directions. No wonder he was in a hurry to get away. Who wouldn't leave, after seeing what a mess she had made of her life?

And she had pushed him by talking about love. She groaned. What had she been thinking? Had she returned to her old ways without meaning to? She prayed that she hadn't.

Kassia felt a deep, burning desire to pray. Not just a plea for help or a quick petition sent up thanking God for another day, but a yearning to talk to Him as her Father, her Redeemer, her creator.

Remembering how she had always gotten on her knees before the Lord each night at bedtime when she was a child, she wondered how it would feel to return to her childlike ways. A long-forgotten passage from Matthew came to her mind: *"I tell you the truth, unless you change and become like little children, you will never enter the kingdom of heaven. Therefore, whoever humbles himself like this child is the greatest in the kingdom of heaven."*

"Okay, Lord. I hear You."

When she was a child, Kassia waited until she was ready for bed before she knelt to pray. Because of this habit, she thought God somehow required His worshippers to wear pajamas when they prayed. Kassia knelt beside her bed and leaned her elbows on the side of her mattress. Now she knew better. God listened to prayers no matter when they were said or what the person communicating with Him was wearing.

Still donned in her dressy pants, red blouse, and high heels, she lowered herself to her knees and leaned her elbows on the bed. She clasped her hands together and bowed her head until her forehead touched her fingers then closed her eyes.

"Lord, please forgive me for straying from You. Thank You for bringing Teague into my life to show me I need to return to You. I know I don't deserve him, Lord, and because of that it may not be Your will for Teague and me to have a relationship beyond friendship. But whatever Your plans are for us, I want to come back to You."

Kassia stayed on her knees for a few moments, drinking in the silence around her that felt permeated with the beauty of the Lord. In her humble act, she was surrendering her will and her own desires so she could be free to wait on the Lord's will for her life. Even though she didn't have a clear sense of the Lord's answer then and there, she felt He accepted her. She felt a leading. That was all she needed.

❧

The following Sunday, Kassia was surprised by a knock on the door. She was thankful she was presentable enough to receive a caller. She had already applied her makeup and slipped on a comfortable long-sleeved turtleneck dress. Feeling sentimental, she had searched her jewelry box and found the simple gold cross Grandma and Grandpa had given her as a high school graduation gift. The cross looked perfect against the solid background.

She slid her feet into her black pumps and hurried to see

who would be visiting on a Sunday morning. Surely it wouldn't be Brad. She doubted he'd be pushy enough or possess enough get-up-and-go to rise early on his day off and drive across town to harass her. He hadn't dropped by her office at work, either, although she had seen him from a distance in the cafeteria.

Kassia peered through the peephole and saw Teague. "Thank You, Lord," she whispered then opened the door.

Immediately she noticed he wasn't using crutches and the cast was missing. Unable to contain herself, she jumped up and down like a little girl and clapped her hands. "Teague! You got the cast taken off!"

"I sure did." He beamed. "I think you're almost as happy as I am."

"I know what a long, hard road it's been for you."

"You're right. This is the first time I've felt normal in quite awhile."

"I know you didn't come all this way on a Sunday morning to show me your cast—or, should I say, lack thereof."

He raised his eyebrows. "Weren't you expecting me?"

"I don't think so, but I'm glad you stopped by."

"I'm here to take you to church. Remember? You promised me you'd let me tag along with you to see what your new church is like."

"Oh, I did promise to, didn't I? I guess I didn't know we'd decided when. But today is perfect. Come on in." She stepped aside for him to enter. "Won't they miss you at your church?"

"I've already been to the eight-thirty service."

"Oh! My, you're ambitious."

He chuckled. "No, I wouldn't say that."

"Well, for being such a good missionary and making sure I don't miss church, the least I can do is treat you to a home-cooked meal after the service," Kassia offered. "You'll let me do that, won't you? I have a Cornish game hen that won't take long to roast."

"Sounds good. Only I beat you to it. I put together a lasagna last night—my first ever. It's my mom's recipe, so it should be safe. Come over to my place for lunch after church, and we can talk while it bakes."

"You can cook? This I have to see!"

He cooked for me!

She laughed nervously. Whatever he wanted to talk about, it must be important.

&

To Kassia's delight, the worship service proved to be as energetic and uplifting as usual. She could see in his eager attentiveness that Teague was impressed by the contemporary music and the sermon about believing without seeing, Jesus' lesson for His disciple Thomas. His unspoken approval made Kassia feel good.

Later the two of them sat at his dining room table as the enticing aroma of lasagna baking filled the home. Kassia sipped a cup of hot tea while she waited for dinner, realizing she felt comfortable as she did whenever she was with Teague. Seeing him working in the kitchen earlier left her feeling gratified that she had helped him through a difficult time. Visions of living that way for the rest of her life danced through her head.

"I have some good news on the job front," he said. "My boss called me this week and begged me to come back."

"Really?" Her eyes widened, and a big smile spread over her face. "So you got the contract reinstated?"

"No, but they did make a successful bid with another company. He was so grateful when I agreed to return that he promised me a raise in pay and even a signing bonus." Teague smiled.

"A signing bonus? Even if you're not new?"

"Yes, and I'm glad for it. Now I can get completely caught up on my bills."

"That's wonderful!" Kassia exclaimed. "I'd say you have a happy ending after all. I'm so glad to hear it."

"I can't help but think the whole thing was the Lord's timing," Teague observed. "He had other things for me to do."

"And I'll bet you appreciate your work now more than ever, since you've been bored at home for so long," Kassia added jokingly.

"And while we're on that subject, can you forgive me?"

"Forgive you? For what?"

"For doubting you."

"You had doubts about me?" Her voice was teasing, but then she spoke quietly. "I think it's only natural for two people to have doubts about each other at first. If you want to know the truth, I was a little scared of you when we first met, too."

"You were?"

She nodded. "I could see how close you were to God, and I wasn't ready to go back to Him. But you led me back."

"Kassia, you sought Him out on your own, and now you glow in the light of His love."

"Is it that obvious?"

"Yes, it is. When I first saw you at Theo's wedding, I couldn't believe how beautiful you were. I never thought you could be more beautiful than you were then. But today you're lovelier than any woman I've ever seen." He reached over and took her hands in his. "The Lord answered my prayers. He sent the perfect woman for me. I love you, Kassia. I don't want to lose you. Ever."

"I love you, too, Teague." Kassia became aware of her pounding heart. "Your love is the answer to my prayer, too. I know now that if I ask Him, and not myself, what to do in life, He will lead me. The Lord knows where we are at all times. We just have to ask Him into our hearts to find our way home."

Teague rose from his seat, and Kassia stood beside him. "I

think we have both listened to the leading of the Lord. Now we can't argue with His will, can we?"

"Of course not!"

He took her in his arms with a gentle yet firm motion. Each became conscious of the other's warmth, of their beating hearts, as they drew together, forming a perfect fit. Kassia felt as though she had spent years wandering in a spiritual desert; only after surrendering her will to the Lord had she found her way home to Him and to the man He had planned for her to walk with on the earth. Teague brought his lips to hers, touching them softly and then with strength, much as their love had strengthened. She knew she would feel the shelter of his love forever.

epilogue

Three Years Later

Kassia sat on the brown leather sofa in the family room of their new house near the city. She laid her hand on her expanding belly and felt it jump. The baby inside her—Teague Junior or little Kathy—kicked with gusto, reminding Kassia she would soon be a mother.

So much had changed since she and Teague wed the previous year. Over time her family had seen that Kassia's transformation was genuine. Even Deidre had softened, visiting as often as she could and presenting Kassia with gifts for the new baby. Mona had since become engaged to her college sweetheart and asked Kassia to be a bridesmaid in her wedding. To Kassia's surprise and delight, Mona had involved her in the dress-selection process.

Instead of dreading her mother's phone calls, Kassia found she looked forward to the time when Mother would be with the new family for a week or so to help them after the baby's birth in June. And when Father saw Teague's new computer game in action, he couldn't deny his son-in-law's talent.

Teague came into the room carrying two glasses of freshly squeezed lemonade. "This should satisfy that craving for something tart." He handed her a glass and sat beside her.

"Thanks. You're too good to me, Teague."

"I haven't forgotten how I was laid up with my ankle. Now it's my turn." He placed his hand on her belly. "And this little one deserves his—or her—mother to receive the best treatment she can." Teague kissed her on the lips. Only his briefest touch left her feeling even better than the first time they kissed—a sensation of love she never thought she could top.

She took a sip of lemonade. "This is great! You make the best lemonade." She smiled, looking into his eyes. "Ouch!"

Teague started right along with her. "Ouch? That sure was a change of mood."

"Sorry. The baby kicked."

"I can see by the way your stomach's moving." He leaned down and spoke into one of the gold buttons on her red maternity dress as though it were a microphone. "Hey! You in there! You can play soccer when you get out. It won't be much longer."

Kassia laughed. "Who says we have a soccer player? Maybe we have a dancer."

"Hey!" Teague said to the baby. "Are you a dancer or a soccer player?" Grinning, he sat back up but kept his hand on her tummy. Within seconds, the baby kicked twice.

"Uh-oh," Kassia said. "We're going to be busy with soccer and dance lessons. I think whoever it is wants to be both."

"Soccer, dance, or both," Teague said. "I love whoever God wants this person to be. And his or her mother."

Kassia felt her eyes mist. "And I love this baby's father, too. And I always will."

KASSIA'S CREAMED POTATOES

5 pounds of russet or red bliss potatoes
8 ounces plain sour cream
1 stick butter
salt and pepper to taste
paprika as optional garnish

Peel potatoes and cut them into quarters. Boil in a heavy pan of water until potatoes are soft. Drain water. Add sour cream and butter that has been sliced to hasten melting. Mash with a potato masher. Whip with electric beaters until lumps disappear. Add salt and pepper. If serving family style in a bowl, top with a sprinkle of paprika for a festive look.

A Letter To Our Readers

Dear Reader:

In order that we might better contribute to your reading enjoyment, we would appreciate your taking a few minutes to respond to the following questions. We welcome your comments and read each form and letter we receive. When completed, please return to the following:

Fiction Editor
Heartsong Presents
PO Box 719
Uhrichsville, Ohio 44683

1. Did you enjoy reading *Forever Friends* by Tamela Hancock Murray?
   ❏ Very much! I would like to see more books by this author!
   ❏ Moderately. I would have enjoyed it more if

   _____

   _____

   _____

2. Are you a member of **Heartsong Presents**?   ❏ Yes   ❏ No
   If no, where did you purchase this book? _____

   _____

3. How would you rate, on a scale from 1 (poor) to 5 (superior), the cover design? _____

4. On a scale from 1 (poor) to 10 (superior), please rate the following elements.

   ____ Heroine   ____ Plot
   ____ Hero   ____ Inspirational theme
   ____ Setting   ____ Secondary characters

5. These characters were special because?_____

_____

_____

6. How has this book inspired your life?_____

_____

_____

7. What settings would you like to see covered in future
   Heartsong Presents books? _____

_____

_____

8. What are some inspirational themes you would like to see
   treated in future books? _____

_____

_____

9. Would you be interested in reading other **Heartsong
   Presents** titles? ❏ Yes ❏ No

10. Please check your age range:
    ❏ Under 18   ❏ 18-24
    ❏ 25-34   ❏ 35-45
    ❏ 46-55   ❏ Over 55

Name_____

Occupation _____

Address _____

City_____ State_____ Zip_____

Sweet Treats

4 stories in 1

*T*hese four complete novels follow the culinary adventures—and misadventures—of Cynthia and three of her culinary students who want to stir up a little romance.

Four seasoned authors blend their skills in this delightful compilation: Wanda E. Brunstetter, Birdie L. Etchison, Pamela Griffin, and Tamela Hancock Murray.

Contemporary, paperback, 368 pages, 5 ³/₁₆" x 8"

❤ ❤ ❤ ❤ ❤ ❤ ❤ ❤ ❤ ❤ ❤ ❤ ❤ ❤

❤ ❤ ❤ ❤ ❤ ❤ ❤ ❤ ❤ ❤ ❤ ❤ ❤ ❤

JHEARTSONG ❤ PRESENTS

Love Stories Are Rated G!

That's for godly, gratifying, and of course, great! If you love a thrilling love story but don't appreciate the sordidness of some popular paperback romances, **Heartsong Presents** is for you. In fact, **Heartsong Presents** is the premiere inspirational romance book club featuring love stories where Christian faith is the primary ingredient in a marriage relationship.

Sign up today to receive your first set of four, never-before-published Christian romances. Send no money now; you will receive a bill with the first shipment. You may cancel at any time without obligation, and if you aren't completely satisfied with any selection, you may return the books for an immediate refund!

Imagine. . .four new romances every four weeks—two historical, two contemporary—with men and women like you who long to meet the one God has chosen as the love of their lives. . .all for the low price of $10.99 postpaid.

To join, simply complete the coupon below and mail to the address provided. **Heartsong Presents** romances are rated G for another reason: They'll arrive Godspeed!

YES! Sign me up for Heart❤ng!

NEW MEMBERSHIPS WILL BE SHIPPED IMMEDIATELY!
Send no money now. We'll bill you only $10.99 post-paid with your first shipment of four books. Or for faster action, call toll free 1-800-847-8270.

NAME_____

ADDRESS_____

CITY_____STATE_____ZIP_____

MAIL TO: HEARTSONG PRESENTS, P.O. Box 721, Uhrichsville, Ohio 44683
or visit www.heartsongpresents.com